ON THE OTHER SIDE

PRAISE FOR THE BOOK

'Love and hatred, romance and flirtations, fake and genuine . . . all so bluntly portrayed . . . a seemingly voluminous narrative written with stunning precision . . . Rahman Abbas's novel [is] a masterpiece. The tongue-in-cheek humour succeeds in artistically camouflaging this harsh and audacious account concerning a community that is more known for *sher-o-shairi*'—Damodar Mauzo, winner of the Jnanpith Award, 2022

'We warm instantly to Abdus-Salam Kalshekar, irate schoolteacher and insatiably amorous adventurer, who is the unlikely hero of Rahman Abbas's novel *On the Other Side*. Kalshekar compels our attention as he negotiates his unconventional way through a conservative Bombay Muslim milieu, quarrelling with God and summing up his fellow human beings in cruel, impatient judgements. Books nest within books in Rahman's adroitly constructed narrative, which takes the form of an extended report by an unnamed writer who is researching Kalshekar's life, to write a novel about him. This maverick, meanwhile, is caught in the act of composing a multi-volume autobiographical testimony to his various love affairs and passionate encounters. Like a painter, Rahman vividly conjures up his protagonist's ethos, with its intimate religious fears and bold secular transgressions. The red thread that stitches the book together is Rahman's inquiry into the art of fiction, its role in contemporary Urdu literature and, by implication, in the India of the troubled present. *On the Other Side* is a loving, lavish, deeply compassionate portrait of an individual, a community and a society caught up in processes of rapid, disorienting transition'—Ranjit Hoskote, poet, cultural theorist and curator

'An astonishingly modern voice, one that needs to be read to understand the crosscurrents in contemporary Urdu fiction'—Rakhshanda Jalil, writer, translator and literary historian

'At its heart, *On the Other Side* is a love story—or, rather, a story about passion. Humorous and philosophical in equal measure, the strength of this book lies in its unabashed portrayal of human relationships'—Hansda Sowvendra Shekhar, author of *The Adivasi Will Not Dance*

'Told through the absorbing and poignant journey of self-discovery of Abdus-Salam in the city of Mumbai, *On the Other Side* is a searing tale of the complexities of human psyche and an exquisite treatment of the beguilingly engaging paradoxes of Indian Muslim life, a masterpiece of universal importance!'—Ashwani Kumar, author of *Banaras and the Other*

'This novel is bold on the grounds of its theme, and complex on the grounds of its narrative technique . . . Abdus-Salam's character, despite his scattered temperament, dishevelled state and stained thoughts, makes a lasting impression on the readers' minds by virtue of his peerless sacrifice. There is no doubt that amid the surge of ordinary novels, this novel is successful in creating its own space and identity as an unconventional, distinct work'—Salam Bin Razzaq, Sahitya Akademi Award-winning author

'It brings to mind Hemingway's *Old Man and the Sea* by virtue of its brevity, but it will be remembered for years in Urdu literature for its theme. It is a major novel of recent years'—Musharraf Alam Zauqi, winner of the Majlis-e-Frogh-e-Urdu Adab Award (Qatar's annual award for contribution to Urdu literature)

'Through this novel, Rahman has bequeathed a unique character to Urdu fiction. To shape a distinctive character is an immense literary feat, which he has accomplished admirably. Rahman's novel embraces the political, religious and societal characters of contemporary society with such proficiency that there is no trace of stagnation or repetition even for a moment. This novel is an important literary achievement'—Paigham Aafaqi, Urdu novelist

'The novel is short, but the conversations it initiates are big . . . and the domain of its thought and vision even larger, which compels us to reflect upon the structure of the novel as well'—Ali Ahmad Fatemi, Urdu critic

ON THE OTHER SIDE

Rahman Abbas

Translated from the Urdu
by RIYAZ LATIF

VINTAGE
An imprint of Penguin Random House

VINTAGE

Vintage is an imprint of the Penguin Random House group of companies
whose addresses can be found at global.penguinrandomhouse.com

Published by Penguin Random House India Pvt. Ltd
4th Floor, Capital Tower 1, MG Road,
Gurugram 122 002, Haryana, India

| Penguin
Random House
India

First published in Vintage by Penguin Random House India 2024

ISBN 9780143465614

Typeset in Bembo MT Pro by MAP Systems, Bengaluru, India
Printed at Thomson Press India Ltd, New Delhi

www.penguin.co.in

For Mahira and Rumi

Ye kaaenat hai meri hi khaak ka zarra
mein apne dasht se guzra to bhed paye bahut
jo motiyon ki talab ne kabhi udaas kiya
to hum bhi raah se kankar samet laye bahut
bas ek raat thaharna hai kya gila kijye
musafiron ko ghanimat hai ye saray bahut
                                        —Shakeb Jalali

This world is but a particle of my dust
many a mystery lay bare when through my
wasteland I passed
the desire for pearls whenever it saddened
we too, then, gathered many pebbles from
the path
why whine, just for a night we have to halt
for the travellers, this inn is blessing
                                        —Shakeb Jalali

'Go to the heart of the matter, and do not allow your mind to linger on who said it or who the person is.'

—Hazrat Ali

'The more one immerses into the recognition of the world, the more one becomes disinterested in it.'

—Hazrat Usman Ghani

More
they read
less
they know
more
pages turned
more
sins committed

—Shah Abdul Latif
(Translated by Anju Makhija
and Hari Dilgir)

'If you had died young, I would have asked you to get life. But you lived long. So I shall ask you to come again the way you came before.'

—Chinua Achebe, *Things Fall Apart*

The muezzin recited the *takbeer*, and the faithful gathered in rows for the Friday prayer. Abdus-Salam Kalshekar too joined them. He was bareheaded. His hair was dishevelled. When the imam began to recite the opening verse of the Quran (*Surah al-fatiha*), Abdus-Salam's ear, at that very instant, began to itch. He resolutely scratched it, and during the act recalled that for days he had been forgetting to buy cotton buds for cleaning the ears. He issued a silent reminder to himself that he would certainly buy them today. As he did so, his eyes wandered to the clock hanging on the wall of the mosque, its hands displaying thirty-five minutes past one. He instantly glanced at his wristwatch, which showed forty-five minutes past one. This discrepancy in time

1

somehow weighed heavily on him. He wondered why clocks in mosques customarily ran late. He wanted to reflect on this realization with gravity, but at that very moment, a big red ant began to crawl along his toe. He lightly jerked his foot a few times to get rid of the ant. Still crawling, however, the ant reached his heel. He was barely able to rein in this calamity when the sanctimonious man beside him stared at him piercingly through the corner of his eye. When their eyes met, he, through a gesture of his eyes, chastised Abdus-Salam that his unwavering concentration ought to be on the imam sahib. Abdus-Salam bowed his head in consternation. Again, his gaze centred on the ant, which had hurled him into a peculiar perplexity. At last, he slowly lifted one foot and rubbed it across the other and found deliverance from the diabolical ant.

The recitation of the Surah al-fatiha concluded, the air resounded with exclamations of amen. He too audibly uttered amen. The instant amen rolled off his tongue, a tender smile illumined his face . . . Amina had sailed into his memory. During his student years, he used to take her to the flourishing shrubbery behind the college, passionately telling her that sweet expressions of love ought to be exchanged where no one else except lush nature would be able to hear them. Amina had been his classmate in the eleventh grade. With Amina's memory, her entire form became resplendent in his mind's eye, where there was a rhythmic resonance of attraction, innocence, intoxication and glow. Then, he was oblivious to when and how the prayer ended. All he kept recollecting were the sweet moments of the days spent with Amina. After the prayers, the imam sahib began to recite benedictions, which were replete with exhortations to the

Almighty to protect the lives and properties of Muslims. Strangely, at that moment, he let out a laugh that he could not prevent. It was anyway evident from his expression that he was not a partaker in seeking benedictions along with the imam. His gaze, however, was fixed on the imam. Unexpectedly, he remembered the imam sahib of his childhood days who frequently detained his friend Nazeer Umar Sheikh after madrasa to have him massage his feet. The imam sahib was a Bangladeshi and was typically draped in a lungi. Fearful of imam sahib's cane, Nazeer Umar Sheikh began to seek refuge in his lungi while massaging his feet. For several years, the sharp whiff of betel leaf, laced with '120 tobacco', a brand that the imam sahib consumed, seemed to waft from Nazeer's body. Some friends from school even told Abdus-Salam that Nazeer Umar Sheikh also reeked of olive oil, which the imam sahib applied to his head. In a guarded, secretive manner, a friend told him that once when he whispered something in Nazeer's ear, he could smell the perfume *jannat al-firdaws* rising from his ear. It was the same perfume that the imam sahib daubed on to a cotton ball and wedged in his left ear. The imam sahib had also stressed to the children that the use of perfume was very worthy from a religious point of view. The crux of the matter is that Nazeer could not continue his studies beyond the introductory primer for the Quran. And then, God knows what possessed him that, stuffing his clothes into a sack, he stepped out of his house and disappeared into the labyrinth of Mumbai No. 8, where the largest flesh-trade bazaar in this tyranny-ridden city has flourished for ages, and whose spread is famously known as Kamathipura to the people at large. The sudden disappearance of Nazeer was a riddle. Abdus-Salam has mentioned Nazeer Umar Sheikh in his private diary only once. But after a couple of years, the enigmatic mist surrounding Nazeer's abrupt disappearance had cleared for him.

With this flash of memory, Abdus-Salam's hands, raised in supplication, fell to cover his face. An inexplicable despondency began to churn in his soul. He got up and stepped out of the precincts of the mosque.

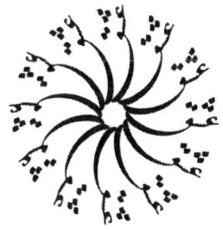

Abdus-Salam was employed as an English teacher in an institution named Anjuman-e-Muslimeen where a great deal of emphasis was laid on instilling and expanding religious values. Scarfs were mandatory for girls. Even while playing kabaddi, boys could not commit the sacrilege of taking off their skullcaps. They were told that if they did, God would abandon them. Abdus-Salam would be astounded when he saw boys from both teams wearing white and black skullcaps, protective amulets and talismans tied to their arms and ankles. At such times he would muse: On whom shall God bestow victory now? Would God be confused in this situation? Then he would tell himself that the Almighty would align Himself with the powerful, for the Almighty was the most intimate with the essence of power.

The teaching staff of the school comprised five men and fifteen women. The female teachers would arrive at the school clad in burkas, and then take them off within the premises. They claimed that the staff room was hot and stuffy. To Abdus-Salam, some of these female teachers themselves were instrumental in making the staff room 'hot'. Over time, the male teachers had acquired an effeminate tenor in their intonation. Their long beards, however, allowed no room for misperception about their male identity. In their free time, they would engage in conversation with the female teachers about matters ranging from the reasons for the decline in religion and faith and the educational backwardness of Indian Muslims to the partisan attitude of the police during riots. The female teachers, in the midst of their stitching and crochet-work, or while savouring fritters and samosas, or while checking students' notebooks, would listen indulgently to their banter. All of them had a gripe against Abdus-Salam that he steered clear of participating in their discussions on such grave and sensitive issues; he had no compassion for society. He would ordinarily be absorbed in a newspaper or a book, with a soft smile on his lips. All the female teachers concurred that students whose medium of instruction was English became proficient in reading and writing far more rapidly compared to the students in Urdu-medium schools. It is on these grounds that they deemed it appropriate to educate their children in English schools. This was the sole area of agreement among the female teachers; otherwise they routinely contradicted one another on most other issues.

Dearth of time, burden of work, stratagems to save money from their salaries so the in-laws would not be able to raise objections, smooth and coquettish guiles for the fulfilment of demands imposed on husbands, were condoms permitted or forbidden? Does pleasure escalate or diminish when using this rubber contraption conceived by the British and Jews? Is there a Zionist conspiracy behind its creation? These were some of the issues on which the female teachers argued intensively when alone, and as was their wont, would never be in accordance with one another. It is possible that they indulged in these arguments solely to amuse themselves. God knows! On the other hand, those among them who were immersed in extramarital liaisons conferred with each other furtively about how much they should squander on their paramours. What gifts should they lavish upon them? Which hotels afforded them inexpensive rooms? Which hotels were sufficiently far away from the city to be safe to spend time there? Often, they would speak candidly about sex, inquiring as to who had experienced the most luscious orgasms. What all should be done to achieve orgasms? Hand-in-hand, they would also exchange notes about who prayed all the special prayers on the holy nights such as *shab-e-qadr* and *shab-e-me'raj*, and who fasted for how many days during the holy month.

Abdus-Salam had surmised that the female teachers were engaged in the process of extracting paramount pleasure and delight from life; whereas the male teachers, decimating and annulling their individuality, shackled to the inevitability of becoming like everyone else, were steadily morphing into innocuous, faceless human beings. He would be bewildered on observing that even the clothes they donned were featureless, lest they reveal any element of individuality. 'The act of eking out an existence within the straightjacketed dictates of community and society has turned most male teachers into *gandu-aadmi,* lily-assed catamites.' He inscribed this line in his notebook, and then, after mulling over it a bit, struck off the words 'gandu aadmi'. In their place, he wrote 'non-human'. He had expunged those words because this notebook was kept in the staff room, and he was worried that if a colleague accidently came across those words in the notebook, it would be unnecessarily hurtful. In Abdus-Salam's assessment, a teacher was a creature who had no identity of his own, no personality, no individuality. He always wanted to look like others. He wanted people to look upon him as a good human being, as an educated human being, and to respect him. For this very reason, he transformed into a meek species, which executed every governmental diktat with a bowed head. He ran away from asking questions. At official functions, he perched like a frog but never offered a contrary opinion on anything. He performed clerical duties for the administration during elections, censuses and other such extraneous events or occasions. In Abdus-Salam's view, a teacher was an entity whose chemistry harboured no trace of critical thought, innovative inquiry, indignation or rebellion.

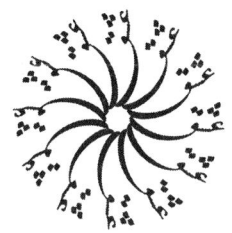

Abdus-Salam was born in Mumbai, and he took great pride in this fortuitous occurrence. No other city had the exalted place that Mumbai had in his heart. His formative years were spent in Andheri, Char Bangla, Saat Bangla and Versova. It was there that his close friends and a host of sweethearts resided. It was there that he had expended the memorable days of his youth.

The members of his household and extended family would offer prayers on Fridays and during the month of Ramazan. They regarded their faith as the sole bearer of Truth and all other religions of the world as errant. He had acquired his early education at a government school in Andheri, where along with textbooks and notebooks, milk, bread and biscuits were distributed every day to the schoolchildren during the recess hours. This was one of the prime reasons that he liked his school. The teachers would offer Friday prayers with the utmost commitment, and on each of these days, immediately prior to the prayers and a little after, Abdus-Salam would keep gazing at the skullcaps on their heads. He had frequently heard the algebra teacher insist that if a Muslim missed offering prayers for three successive Fridays, he would be regarded as excommunicated from the sphere of Islam. Consequently, Abdus-Salam would skip his prayers for two weeks but would diligently make up for them on the third Friday. This arrangement ossified into a habit for the rest of his life.

He could recite numerous benedictions and holy verses from memory, but oddly enough, it was confounding to try and fathom wholly his thoughts on matters of religion. Every so often, he came across as exceedingly grave about religion, but then frequently, it seemed as if religion was nothing but a mask. It is possible that he was not amenable to exhibiting his inner spiritual self. But his thoughts, with which his close friends were familiar, embraced the notion that in the epoch in which he breathed, religion was merely a means to shroud the inferior-most visage of the self. It was the armament of self-promoting, ostentatious people. Religion could not be a measure of individuals being good or bad. Mindless folks with irrational brains were not capable of comprehending the aesthetic splendour of religion. Could those who were not acquainted with the profound meaningfulness of sexuality and beauty be close to God?

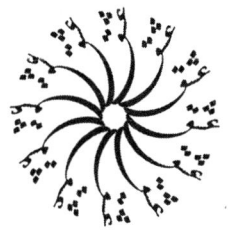

On the other hand, it was amusing to see that if even a common ailment cast its faint shadow over him, he would rush to the mosque and make supplications to God: 'Ya Allah, I kept entertaining blasphemous thoughts about You . . . Are you punishing me for it? Whatever I think, it is not I who thinks it; my brain conjures up everything. What can I do? However irreverent this brain is, it is You who have created it. If even a tiny leaf cannot move without Your command, what can this unworthy brain do? Is it at all probable (he would try to plunge into deep contemplation) that You are the one inciting me to think against You, in the same manner that You provided divine guidance to Lucifer to open up a rebellious front against You? This is all

Your game. Okay, I shall henceforth never think critically about You . . . but You will have to provide me with divine guidance.' He would step out of the mosque blissful and content after this supplication. If a triumphal feeling arose in his heart, he would order *maava*, a tobacco-based medley, from the paan shop: Bhola tambaku, katri supari, star mar kar (a mix of lime paste, raw betel nut shavings and some star anise).

Stuffing the maava in his mouth, he would stroll about. He would not remove his skullcap. Exchanging pleasantries with people on the neighbourhood's streets, he would roam the bazaar. Soon enough, when he descended from his heady crest, he would muse: The one to whom I addressed so many supplications . . . does He even exist? Or is it merely my delusion? What can a man do . . . helpless as he is? After a pause, he would resume his thoughts: It was not an issue if God did not exist . . . but what if He did? He would meditate upon the existence of God for a bit longer and then state: One's welfare lies in not working against Him (then do whatever pleases you as everyone does) . . . But each time, at this juncture, he would shake his head in negation and conclude his soliloquy with himself on this thought: What will remain if I too become like everyone else? No, no! I cannot indulge in deception with my breath-soul. *'Mein Apne Nafs Ka Izhar Hun'* ('I am Merely a Manifestation of My Being') is the sub-title of his personal diary.

According to Abdus-Salam, God is everyone's shield, and surreptitiously, He spends a little bit of time with everyone. Ogadia, Dvani and Maududi, they all have a God. Laden, Saddam and Mulla Omar, they all have a God. George Bush, Putin and Tony Blair, they all have a God. Madonna,

Madhuri and Karishma, they all have a God. He often says that man thinks that until he is not viewed with respect by others, he is a lesser man. According to him, the human mind had not yet developed the ability to think about this issue differently.

'At least for five million years more, in severing themselves from God, human beings may not be in a position to make a collective effort to discover themselves. Or perhaps never. But then, man does not remain bound to God either. He wears God like a shalwar; applies Him like vermillion on the forehead or puts Him on like a skullcap. Or as around a shrine, he arranges qawwalis around Him. He exploits God in order to seize for himself a suitable place in society, for acceptance. It is as if in this desert of existence, God were a covering sheet that would be above our heads eternally. We fear that the moment we step out of His shade, the delicate fibres of our heart will melt in the intensity of the infernal heat.'

The paragraph above featured in the second chapter, 'Memoir of Man', in the manuscript of his first novel, *Unpublished*. But this paragraph is missing in the edition that was published. He had expunged the paragraph in the manuscript itself. He was apprehensive that his views would offend his religious friends (who were all litterateurs). Deleting the paragraph, he had jotted on the margins with a pencil: 'I cannot reveal even those things about You to others that You Yourself wish for me to reveal to them.'

Abdus-Salam would occasionally express boundless faith in God, while at other times, he would be greatly vexed at Him. Sometimes, in rage and indignation, he would censure Him for His erroneous decrees and for being with the untrue congregation of the faithful or the wrong *jamaat*. Then he would reason: 'Dude, when You do not exist, why do I nail all these accusations on You? Am I out of my mind?' Then he would smile and say: 'Listen! If You exist, do not exact retribution from me for my worthless and nonsensical utterings.' Looking up at the sky, he would mutter such phrases in his heart.

In the context of his monologue with himself, when someone would inquire what the matter was, he would reply: 'I am seeking absolution from the Creator. May God safeguard you too from immodesty and malevolence.'

The minute the curious enquirer was on his way, he would grin and mumble: '*Inna lillahi wa inna ilayhi raji'un*' (from God are we and to Him shall we return; this verse is usually recited on the news of someone's demise or if a natural calamity takes place). 'What a line-up of clowns You have created!'

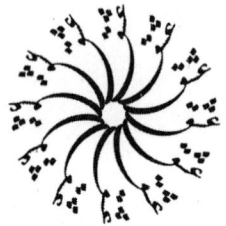

One day, Abdus-Salam's rage at God burst for the first and the last time upon one of his students. As it happened, the school had organized an excursion to some hilly region. The landscape resounded with the sound of water rushing forth from a waterfall. The students as well as teachers were absorbed in fun and frolicking. Settled in the shade beneath a tree, Abdus-Salam was reminiscing about a picnic from the days of his youth when steering a girl named Shehla to a thick grove behind the trees, he had begun to expound upon the contours of passion and love to her. Emerging from the ruins of the past, the lust-laden vistas of that evening were just about to become resplendent on his mind's screen, when a student who routinely posed facetious questions on solemn matters approached him and aired his question: 'Sir, where does the water in this waterfall come from?'

A virulent, heart-cleaving utterance issued from Abdus-Salam's tongue. The boy squirmed and instantly disappeared from his presence. After a while, Abdus-Salam felt remorse for his conduct. He recalled that he had recently read in a book that each utterance delivered by our tongue circles over us for numerous years. Those amongst us who are supremely sensitive can even hear the echoes of those utterances. Some of our utterances are such that they wait in interminable voids for the time when we shall be bound to tender our dues for those statements.

Under the tree, for a long time, he kept seeking out his past beloved in his heart's maze but she did not appear. But yes, after that day, Abdus-Salam rigorously avoided making eye contact with that boy. He ignored him. But who knows what substance that wretched student was moulded from! Whenever he spotted Abdus-Salam walking out of the school's mosque after Friday prayers, in the blink of an eye, like some dutiful jinn, he would alight in front of him and greet him: 'Sir, as-salaam-alaikum.' Sometimes, he would add *rahmatullah*, God's mercy, to his greeting. Abdus-Salam would feel as if this greeting was issuing forth not from the boy's mouth, but brimming with vengeance, from the very source of the water in the waterfall.

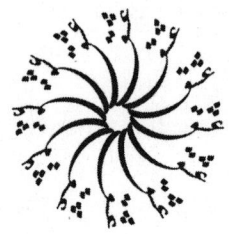

In light of the information that I have gathered, it can be affirmed that people were quite fond of Abdus-Salam. He was friendly in his disposition. Only when some mediocre individual was hyperbolically praised in front of him would he show signs of considerable distress. During an academic function, a lady, during her speech, gushed: 'As great a scientist that he is, the ex-president Mr Mizail Khan is an equally extraordinary poet.' Abdus-Salam could not restrain himself. He rushed to the stage and addressing the lady declared: 'Madam, Mizail Khan's English poetry is of the same (ordinary) calibre as Munawwar Pratap Rana in Urdu.' A roar of laughter spread through the audience to the extent that the gushing lady, too, could not suppress her laughter.

(Munawwar Pratap Rana had passed away just two years ago. He was a local businessman from Mumbai who also dabbled in poetry. Though he was an inferior third-rate poet, he claimed that he was the Ghalib of his age, and all those who called his poetry substandard had no understanding of the art of poetry.) An episode associated with Abdus-Salam, quite similar to the episode inscribed here, had gained considerable renown in the scholarly circles of Mumbai. One of his ustads, a storywriter, was also the editor of a literary journal. Abdus-Salam probably did not like the stories that his ustad wrote. Once, someone among his intimate friends asked him: 'What is your assessment of the ustad's stories?' Without hesitation, he burst out: 'He is a *chutiya* writer.' In a couple of weeks, this remark reached the ears of Abdus-Salam's ustad. Soon, there was a literary gathering where his ustad was present. Abdus-Salam was introducing someone to his teacher: 'Meet him; he is my ustad.' The teacher began to rage: 'On my face you call me your ustad, and behind my back, a chutiya! Now you yourself have become a teacher? Have some shame.'

A few storywriters and poets gathered around them. Abdus-Salam levelled his eyes with his teacher's and said: 'Sir, how can I call you a chutiya? Are you a chutiya?' The gathered writers began to chuckle. Embarrassed, and not really comprehending what had just transpired, the ustad slid to a corner with an awkward smile on his face. Abdus-Salam muttered under his breath: 'Truly, he is such a chutiya.' Until 2003, the expletive chutiya was used in Mumbai for someone who was considered an imbecile. After this incident, people wickedly started using the name of Abdus-Salam's ustad in place of this expletive. During the final years of his life, Abdus-Salam felt exceedingly regretful at the memory of this incident.

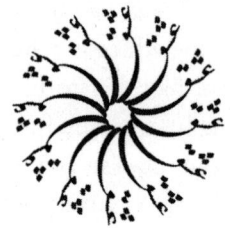

The month of Ramazan was not a month of divine blessings for him; on the contrary, it was filled with torment. He did not fast, but throughout the day, he would assume the state of the devout who were fasting. He would bemoan his condition and frequently say to himself: 'I wish I could reveal to them that I am not fasting. And I am hungry.' When he was at home, he would frequently eat and drink throughout the day, and just before the call to the evening prayer, lodge himself at the table for the evening meal. Reciting holy blessings with his mother, he would 'break' his fast, and then descend and step out of his building along with his brothers. His elder brother would proceed towards the mosque, while he would end up at the paan shop: 'Bhola tambaku, katri supari, star mar kar.'

The shopkeeper would enquire: 'Sir, how are the fasts progressing?'

His reply: 'I can barely feel them this year.'

Putting the paan in his mouth, he would speak in his mind: 'Who the hell does not feel them?' Then looking up at the sky, he would contemplate: 'In this holy month, if You completely restrain Satan, then who is leading me astray? In all likelihood, it is You who does not wish that I fast. If that is Your divine will, why would I be gifted the good sense to keep fasts? In fact, there would have been no harm had I fasted. At school, I anyway go hungry for most hours.' After a while, countering his own train of thought, he would continue: 'What is this insanity! You would be pleased if I went hungry? You can't be that stupid. That is, if at all You exist! But due to fasting, my digestive issues will be resolved. There are numerous advantages of fasting; I shall certainly do it next time. Not for Your sake but for the sake of my stomach.' But such a day never arrived.

The very next day after his fiftieth birthday, when he had a bout of diarrhoea, he said to his doctor: 'I know all too well who is behind all this. If only I had kept those bloody fasts!' Then turning his gaze to the sky, he said in a heartfelt tone: 'Such rigorous retribution against such a feeble man!'

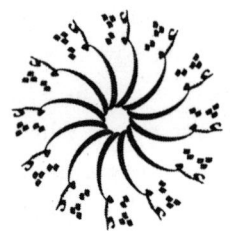

'There is a very substantial group of women-teachers in Indian society who are prey to mental, monetary and sexual discontent, and whose sufferings no one really comprehends.' Abdus-Salam's recurrent repetition of this phrase was an integral part of his experience.

The face these female teachers present at the school is at the antipode of their true selves. Excessive reliance on religion is an expression of the confounded scattering of one's being. Whenever Abdus-Salam entered into a conversation with the burqa-clad teachers, he would also become aware of their tragic disposition. He has written somewhere: 'Often, I have encountered the odour emanating from the bodies of women with sad hearts.' According to him, the reason for this odour was that, due to their melancholic disposition, rashes broke out on these women's bodies, which after a time, becoming fetid, began to discharge pus, the odour of which was not evident to everyone. Frequently, these women themselves were not able to understand the true origins of this odour.

On occasion, he also sensed that among the female teachers who went for prayers in the room adjoining the school staff room there were some who were, in fact, seeking a secluded place to shed tears. The secrets of their minds and bodies had opened up to them. But finding the path to their fulfilment blocked, they were ravaged by agitated wrath. It was thus, that placing their heads in God's lap, they longed to forget their feminine orientation. Those among them whom God refused to clasp to His divine bosom apparently set out once a week or once a fortnight to lend a hand in the completion of the unfinished works of some clerk, some teacher or some neighbour. To provide a numerical sequence to files, help in composing articles, recheck the marks jotted on the examination answer sheets—their immersion in such works was, truth be told, an expression of the most distressing portion of the sad untold story buried in the dungeons of their being.

The above secret, to a great degree, had been revealed to Abdus-Salam. For this very reason, he would be wrapped in a strange feeling of loss on observing these teachers working so devotedly. He knew: 'Work is the vilest weapon to kill time as well as being.' And these deprived teachers were using it. These were the eternally living dead. But Abdus-Salam also had sympathy for them, and it was this very sympathy that took him to the house of the senior-most teacher in the school who had been married for ten or twelve years. Her husband was employed in Saudi Arabia. She had two children, both from this husband. Abdus-Salam watched a movie on the television with her. Then they chatted about their colleagues and staff. Then tea, then jovial banter . . . and then occasionally, there would be conversation in a mystical Sufi mode about the merits and attributes of God, the compassionate, the munificent. As Abdus-Salam began to visit her house more and more frequently, she too moved rapidly from sari to shalwar kameez to a gown. After a few months, once when Abdus-Salam, reclining by her side, extolled to her the benefits of gowns in summers, the senior-most teacher's gown too, like a television, was eyeing him from a corner; it was listening to him talk. Abdus-Salam was at ease; the senior-most was also at ease. From the beginning, they had had a premonition and anticipation about where all this was headed. Their only regret was that they had expended several intermediate weeks in vaulting across the wall of unfamiliarity.

Abdus-Salam's relationship with the senior-most lasted for twenty-six years.

Even after her husband's return and her children's stride into youth, the spectacle of love continued under the guise of friendship. And it ended when senior-most's red scarlet days were taken over by a viscous white flow. Four months into the appearance of the viscous white flow, senior-most filled up the form to undertake the pilgrimage of Haj. Abdus-Salam kept laughing raucously on that day although he had no idea why he was guffawing so hard. Perhaps he knew the reason but did not deem it appropriate to commit it to his diary. When she came to meet him for one final time, Abdus-Salam's tongue, in the desolation of the moment, discharged taciturn sentences: 'May God transfer your sins to my name. My God understands the nature of relationships. He is non-existence.'

Nine years after her return from Haj, and fifteen years before Abdus-Salam's demise, senior-most passed away as a result of heart failure. He too was present among the mourners. Her corpse was kept in another room where women were getting a last glimpse of her with tearful eyes. But Abdus-Salam felt as if he were standing next to the corpse, gazing at senior-most's pale rosy face.

It was as if the corpse were telling him: 'Look, how many deep secrets of this body are buried in your heart? My heart was flooded with your memories and had to explode one day due to frailty.'

Vortices arose in Abdus-Salam's eyes, where there were no tears, but some sand.

He hurriedly left.

Passing through Mohammad Ali Road, he paused at a paan shop.

'Arre yaar, give me a paan—Bhola tambaku, katri supari, star mar kar.'

His tone betrayed melancholy, and it seemed as if vortices of sand were forming in his throat.

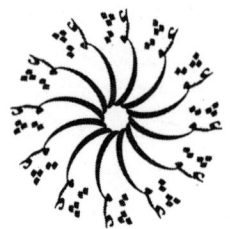

It was Abdus-Salam's long-standing aspiration to finish his *Dastan-e-Ishq*, 'Saga of Passion', before death consumed him. Already, he had manuscripts of three volumes ready, but until all the seven volumes that he had conceived, all the seven that lay secure in his heart, did not become the adornments of paper, he did not wish to publish them. He offered two reasons for this: firstly, his readers would be unfairly subjected to restlessness and discomfort in anticipation of the next volume; secondly, he would have to face the displeasure of all his one-time beloveds (those who were still alive) who did not merit mention in the published works. As a forthright man, he did not want to be, in undue haste, an unwitting perpetrator of injustice on any of his beloveds.

He had resolved to write 'Saga of Passion' in the days when he was a student. Truth be told, it was his girlfriend, Shehla, who had first nudged him towards this. Shehla once said to him: 'This endearing craziness with which you lure me to the bushes behind the college to make out with me under the ruse of showing me birds' nests; will you not release this craziness upon the world? Cannot this passionate madness of ours be celebrated and be immortal in the annals of history?' Then, in a surge of affection, wiping the lipstick off Shehla's lips with a handkerchief that he had whisked out of his pocket, he had replied: 'Our love shall be the most memorable account of the present epoch, which I myself shall write.' After this proclamation, when he centred his gaze on the handkerchief to look at the scarlet-red marks of the lipstick, he stood stunned and confounded. In haste, he had mistakenly stuffed his father's white skullcap in his pocket instead of the handkerchief. It would be disastrous now to take the skullcap back home. He contemplated: 'Why not bequeath the skullcap to the wild bushes as an insignia of love?'

For a few days, this love affair remained at its peak. Then Shehla had an epiphany that it was imperative to part in love otherwise it would not achieve historical loftiness. Probably under the heady influence of this idea, she became amenable to the abandonment of love. Shehla's fickle betrayal turned his heart into an 'indigent's lamp', as a consequence of which he was spotted for a few days in a restless afflicted state, downing endless cups of tea in the canteen, reciting sad couplets of Meer. In time, this sorrow dissipated at the blossoming of an affair with another girl. But the most valuable lesson that the last affair had taught him was that it was vital to inscribe the episodes of love in a diary before going to bed every night so that he would not forget them due to their profusion. In this manner, a distinct diary was to be kept for narratives of amour with each exclusive beloved so that incidents would not get confused with each other, and if there was a similarity in names, he would not commit the folly of thinking them one and the same in the advanced years of his life.

With time, he began to record the episodes of love with firm regularity. He kept these diaries in a special cabinet, which he had tacitly named *Akhri Shab Ke Hamsafar*, 'Fellow-Travellers of the Ultimate Night'. For as long as he stayed with his parents, he kept the keys to the cabinet with himself. Over the span of his life, fifty-three small diaries came to be amassed in his cabinet in which, apart from numerous incidents, marginalia, dates, entries of presents and grievances, his views on the experience and emotion of love are chronicled. He had penned the three manuscripts of 'Saga of Passion' on the foundation of these diaries, which incorporated the material from merely twenty-six diaries. In the yet-to-be-composed four volumes of 'Saga of Passion', he wanted to utilize the narratives of love from the remaining diaries but was not able to bring it to completion due to lack of time as well as an unruliness of disposition. He intended to pursue this work much more industriously after retirement. Whatever expenses would be incurred for the publication of all the seven volumes, he would recompense from the money obtained from his Provident Fund.

In these fifty-three diaries, in addition to some virgin girls, the wives of a few esteemed individuals, four schoolteachers from Mumbai, one young teenage girl, three divorced women, two Gujarati girls, one Keralite girl, one Tamil and four Marathi women, there were the wives of three friends, who featured under pseudonyms so as to prevent undesirable rifts in friendships. He had written about all his amours with intense meticulous toil. But even when he greatly desired, he could not bring himself to mention one particular amour in his diary. A certain beloved who soared over a lengthy interval of his existence, becoming a spire of memory, continued to revisit recurrently the dark alleys of his heart in the midst of his ongoing loves. It would not be inaccurate to say that the girl inhabited a corner of Abdus-Salam's heart, but he routinely made efforts to relegate that corner to oblivion. He could never bring himself to write a diary dedicated to her. Each time, after writing a few lines, he turned sorrowful and morose due to which he would be emotionally scattered for days. He did not possess a remedy for this ripple of grief, nor did he have an explication for, and insight into, this epiphany of love. This was the sole love affair that was impossible to record. A few days before his unexpected death, when he had mused upon the string of his beloveds during a moment of reckoning, he had become resolutely clear that she was the only girl whose story he could not write. But barring her, he had never been steeped in love with anyone else with an absolute surrender of body and soul. It dawned upon him then: 'Words are too frail in the face of the surging force of emotions. Therefore, the episodes of true love are impossible to commit to words.'

He had inscribed these lines on the first page of one of his favourite books. The book was titled *Dagh-e-Ishq Tanha Rah Gaya*, 'The Mark of Passion Stayed Solitary'. He probably inscribed those lines a few months before his death. This is being inferred keeping that book's date of publication in mind.

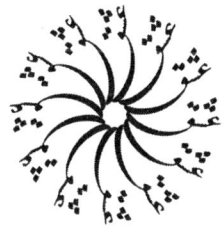

I intend to write a bulky novel on Abdus-Salam's life for which I am gathering material, and on the foundation of which I shall undertake to give a fictional form to his persona and character. For all I know, even I am incapable of recounting the above-mentioned amours. For whatever is inscribed without the veracity of experience is a figment of imagination, and love is a non-fictive, tangible reality. It is our human vulnerability that we are capable of writing about all other occurrences but not about our palpable, real love. In this context, I can certainly reveal this much to you that Abdus-Salam believed that if he had not written diaries dedicated to his beloveds, it is possible many of them would have been erased from his memory, but the one mentioned above was the one solitary love, where in not committing it to words, he had been successful in preserving it in his memory with much greater intensity.

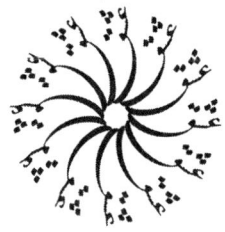

Abdus-Salam was not too fond of Hindi films. However, he would frequently invoke a couple of heroines during conversations. Their intoxicating insatiable bodies, coquetry laced with theatrics, and their exclamations during love scenes (which are lush with desire) were the centre of his curiosity. In light of his experiences, he would assert: 'Women customarily lie corpse-like during lovemaking. This is the peak of psychological coercion perpetrated by the patriarchal society where women, even during their moments of pleasure, end up being numb and lifeless, in fact, turn into a corpse.' He would say: 'Alas, women have been able to learn nothing even after watching the heroines in films. Which means the frost of collective oblivion has permeated their brain cells immeasurably.' Once when a conversation about this subject was in progress and someone asked him that if what he said was true, then it was equally true that the film heroines too were women after all . . . then how did they remember what the song of the soul was during moments of love? After listening attentively, he had said that men retained vividly in their memory the effect that women's sounds of desire had on them, and these love scenes were unconscious expressions of that very memory. At the core, men long to be in the embrace of a woman whose soul's song they can hear. But women have remained so fearful of the patriarchal society that their music inside flickers in their bodies at the reminiscence of men, but invariably becomes a prisoner of self in the presence of men. Some friends vehemently agreed with him. Turning to the three friends who had said to him in one voice, 'What you say holds a lot of weight,' he had impishly whispered: 'Are your wives heroines?' All other friends excluding the three had guffawed raucously at this remark.

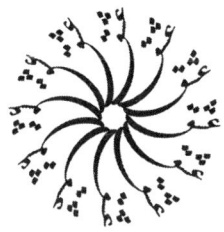

In his judgement, all others barring a few reputed poets kept lamenting about unattainable bodies. He would say: 'These wretches; nor are they immersed in love, nor do they have insights into nature's secrets, nor are they acquainted with religious and economic conflagrations; wonder why they keep toying with rhymes and refrains.' In his opinion, Urdu literature was utterly deprived of the colourful exuberance, freshness and heady moods of love and sex. It was deprived of the depth of the bond between a man and a woman. It was deprived of the possibilities of what effects of love and sex register on the psyche of a man and a woman, and what all they can become to achieve sex and love. The imaginative conception of woman in Urdu poetry was worthless and unrealistic; it was nothing but man's obscene outpouring.

Once, someone asked him: 'What is your opinion about Allama Iqbal?' He was irked: 'He has conned everyone and departed. The exemplary men of God (*mard e-momin*) cannot be made; they are just born. Iqbal's thoughts are all theoretical, not practical. Nonetheless, he is a great poet.'

As far as mushairas or poetic symposiums were concerned, he used to deride them as ignoble pageants, devices for the base amusement of politicians and affluent seths. He used to call the crass poets who regularly performed at these mushairas *bhand,* wretched jesters. He has written somewhere that these poets are animals of a breed in which ninety per cent are foul-natured and disastrous.

And this was his assessment of Urdu fiction writers: 'This is a lone bunch of individuals whom no one knows apart from they themselves; no one recognizes them, no one reads them. They merely read each other's writings and write articles commending each other's works. What can be more foolish than the fact that they flatter themselves by calling each other Kafka and Maupassant but are grossly incompetent at distinguishing between the creative worlds of these two writers.' He would routinely repeat this and laugh uproariously. Then he would resume: 'God too is a storywriter, and he is worse off than these Urdu storywriters. He Himself decrees his books written, Himself decrees them read, and Himself hears them. Following this hearing, He also rewards the readers. What a bizarre drama this is!' Once, during such a conversation, he had said: 'In fact, the greatest tragedy of all is with this celestial storywriter.'

Everyone around him remained silent. Scanning their faces, he said: 'You are all scared. You think, abandoning everything, Khuda, God, will come hunting for you if something unspeakable slips off your tongues. Oh! What pestilences and natural calamities will you have to endure!' His friends still kept silent. At least one friend's face looked sullen. Placing a hand on his shoulder, Abdus-Salam jibed: 'You are right. Neither extended friendship nor enmity with Allah is good.'

His friend grinned.

A smile spread on Salam's face too. Then he silently said in his mind: 'Do you see, Khuda Ji! People consider you like a policeman from Mumbai.'

After a while, at the same spot, wondering in which thought he was lost, a friend asked him: 'Yaar, now what the hell are you thinking about?'

Rising out of a vortex of thoughts then, he said: 'I am admiring God's splendorous spectacle. He has created each thing so proportionately.' His friend immediately gushed: 'Praise be to God!' Some other faces, too, blossomed instantly.

Strolling up to a friend, he inquired softly: 'I said *tanasub*, 'proportionate'. You did not hear something else, I trust . . .?' Then stretching his neck, he looked into his friend's eyes. For a few moments, both of them kept looking at each other in the same state. (God knows if he truly wanted to use the word tanasub, 'proportionate' here, or had some other word in mind laden with the possibility of mischief.

I thought about it once, and a few words came to my mind with the likelihood that he meant some word from among them. Those words were *tanasul* [penis], *tasahul* [carelessness] . . . Or it is entirely possible that this might merely be my erroneous imagination. I have therefore ruled that I will not include these exchanges in the final draft.)

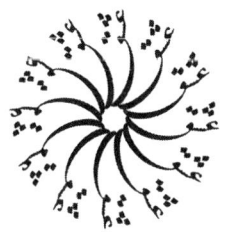

After some time, he landed at the paan shop at the corner of the street: 'Bhola tambaku, katri supari, star mar kar . . . put in all these proportionately.'

'What is proportionately supposed to mean?' the boy at the paan shop asked him.

'Proportionate means whatever is in my fate,' Abdus-Salam replied.

The boy chuckled and said: 'Sahib, you are good at pulling legs.'

Both smiled, and a smoky rancour that was surging in Salam's being receded substantially.

One day:

Since morning, his heart was not at rest, was not interested in any activity. He was enveloped in an odd perplexity. But a contrivance to liberation from inner worthlessness and dispersion was in sight. He boarded the bus from Andheri station and made his way straight to St Mary's church in Mahim. The church was swarming with men, women and children. He managed to make some space for himself and focused on reading the facial expressions of the faithful engrossed in prayers. If his gaze congregated on a pretty girl or woman, he would not be content to merely 'read' the face. He would also savour the feminine form. On his left, a sprightly beautiful woman was immersed in prayer. She had donned a red skirt and a white T-shirt. Eyeing the attractive contours of her face and her shapely legs, Abdus-Salam thought: 'Ill-fated is that creative mind that is deprived of this gift of ecstasy.' At this thought, he recalled a poem by Faiz Ahmed Faiz that he had downloaded from YouTube a few days before. He could summon to memory a couple of lines of the poem:

Haa.e us jism ke kambakht dil-āvez khutūt
Aap hī kahiye kahīñ aise bhī afsūñ hoñge
Apnā mauzu-e-sukhan un ke sivā aur nahīñ
Tab.a-e-shā.er kā vatan un ke sivā aur nahīñ

Oh! the calamitous, heart-riveting contours of this body
Say, would there be such sorcerous charms anywhere?
The object of my words is nothing else but these
The abode of a poet's essence is nothing else but these

As he was murmuring these lines he spotted an old friend, Pankaj, who was a member of the Communist Party of India. Both were friends from their college days. In those days, Pankaj had made concerted efforts to explain Karl Marx's theory to Abdus-Salam. Pankaj was desirous that Abdus-Salam join the Communist Party, represent educated Muslims in the leftist movement, and increase their membership in the party. Abdus-Salam would listen to Pankaj and cast his propositions to the winds. He was acutely aware of the fact that just as he was prey to scepticism about the existence of God, he was also prey to disbelief in the non-existence of God. His nature was not suited to politics. In this regard, he had penned in his personal diary: 'Rather than being stuck in the mire of politics, it is better that I remain submerged in the quicksand of the self.' This is not at all to say that he attempted to flee from the subject of politics; instead, those who have given me valued information about him were of the view that his political consciousness was alert and mature, but he attached greater significance to observing life by staying detached from political and social activism.

Abdus-Salam was surprised at spotting Pankaj in the church. He wondered what Pankaj had come there for. Was it that a possibility had occurred to accommodate God into Karl Marx's theory? Could it be that bloody Marx had morphed into the prophet of Marxism?

Somehow Abdus-Salam managed to reach Pankaj.

He placed his hand on Pankaj's shoulder. Startled, he turned.

On seeing Abdus-Salam, Pankaj was overcome with
a condition that was an admixture of astonishment and
inquest. At first, Abdus-Salam felt as if Pankaj had been
rendered mute, or as if a thorn had been wedged in his
throat. He thought, 'This guy must be thinking that the one
I wanted to turn into a communist, deserting his God, what
is he doing in the holy court of my God?'

A bewildered Pankaj, greeting him, shook hands with
him. The moment Pankaj uttered 'Salaam, yaar,' a wave of
alarm surged through the [Christian] folks around them.
Before things got out of hand and the police were summoned
in panic, both of them stepped out of the church. Walking
silently, they entered a café. To veil their bemusement, they
began to indulge in small talk, making trite enquiries about
each other. After a while, when their amazement receded
a little, they both enquired almost at the same time: 'What
are you doing here?'

And smiles spread across both their faces.

Pankaj said: 'Yaar, my wife is religious, and I come here
from time to time to keep her happy. With other members
of the church, she works for the betterment of street-kids.'
Then, effecting a more solemn tone, he declared: 'But I am
still a communist. I have nothing to do with God-Vod; it
is just for the woman's happiness . . .' Abdus-Salam could
not contain himself, and before Pankaj could complete his
sentence, he interjected: 'A Muslim man does not supplicate
before God for his woman's happiness. For us, it is polytheism.
But by one reckoning, you are fortunate. Our God might
just exculpate an atheist, but not a *mushrik*, a polytheist.' To
explicate what he was saying, he also elucidated to Pankaj

the concepts of *shirk* (attributing a partner to God) and mushrik (one who assigns partners to God).

A faint tint of embarrassment and confusion appeared on Pankaj's face. He smiled again, for smiling is an easy way of making discomfiture fade away, and the use of which the communists are anyway very proficient at making.

'And you tell me, what are you doing in a church? Have you become a Christian or what?' Pankaj asked after some moments.

'Listen, yaar! The one who could not submit to his own religion in totality, how will he submit to the church?'

'You fucker, then what were you doing in the church?'

'You see, this is the thing. It is the month of May. The school is closed for vacations. A gnawing vacuity haunted me at home. So, I thought, let me indulge in some time-pass. Thus, I came here. Here, one can ogle at one superior *maal* after another. Where I live, only black goats are visible.' They both burst into a guffaw. Then again, for a long stretch, they conversed about trifles. Before parting, they exchanged their mobile numbers with the promise to meet soon.

After a few days, Abdus-Salam went to Pankaj's house.

They talked about the current state of affairs, and Pankaj's wife, too, was an equal participant in the conversation. Abdus-Salam was pleased to learn that Pankaj's wife was quite steeped in English literature. Both of them embarked on a discussion about English fiction. Pankaj's wife was in need of some books on 'the philosophical foundations of postmodernism', which were not obtainable. Handing three books on the subject to her, Salam said: 'Those who cannot write, they can live in the labyrinth of linguistics.'

This statement made an enduring impression on Pankaj's wife, and she pledged to herself that she would read only literature and would not waste her time reading superfluous philosophical texts that were composed in the name of literature. In this fashion, a dialogue on literature ensued between them and played a critical role in bringing them to an inevitable intimacy. Once, Salam bought a book for her titled *Memories of My Melancholy Whores*. In the act of handing the book to her, the rouge of her lipstick somehow got on to Salam's handkerchief. On reaching home, when he washed the handkerchief, he was amazed to discover that the rouge mark, spreading further, had turned substantially deeper. He has mentioned this occurrence in his personal diary; he has also transcribed it under the subheading, 'The Rouge of Her Lips' in his 'Saga of Passion'. The colour of the lipstick had its own scent, which Abdus-Salam kept invoking and feeling in the bathroom for several days. Over there, at one end, the comrade [Pankaj] was engaged in his political activities, and here, these two [Salam and Pankaj's wife] were absorbed in the worlds of literature and romance. This state of affairs persisted until the comrade's transfer. The comrade was an employee in a bank as well as a leader of the bank union.

Two or three days before the transfer:

Abdus-Salam had invited the comrade and his wife to his house. An animated exchange took place on issues related to Indian trade unions, the break-up of Soviet Russia, the state of the party in Kerala and Bengal, and leftist literature. After lunch, Pankaj gently succumbed to siesta. As he dozed, Salam steered his wife to his cupboard.

Removing the handkerchief, which still retained the feel of the lipstick's scent, he placed it in her hand.

Witnessing such devotion, the heart-scorched Amrita's eyes clouded over hazily. She concealed the handkerchief and put it in her purse. That evening, Abdus-Salam noted this episode in his diary. Under the title, 'Amrita, if Only You Had Lived A few More Days', he has penned ten pages. These pages register the entries of that heady inebriation that was attained through his conversations with Amrita. In a particular paragraph, he has inscribed that recurrently he feels that a want of intellectual compatibility stands as a crucial reason for the death of relationships. In love, a woman is much more desirous of concord, intimacy, respect and care than sex. The other vital thought he has tendered to those pages stresses that the object of a man's desire is not ordinarily a woman; rather, it is the fulfilment of that very desire. And it is for this reason that man frequently remains deprived of love's majestic essence, whereas woman is a seeker of love, and more often than not, stakes everything for its attainment . . . the dignity of being as well as life itself. In these can be excavated the reasons for woman's evanescence.

In this world, all are not evil, still:

In a society where debased and more debased deeds are perpetrated but their mention is forbidden and virtually sinful, someone like Abdus-Salam was fated to juggle many impediments; it was a society whose roots lay in deceit, falsehood, insidiousness and fulfilment of carnal desires, but absolutely prohibited all freedom of expression. Amidst the tongue that people around him used, in which there was a convention of singing hollow, hoarse songs of morality while casting a veil over the exacting realities of life, it is not too easy to appraise how helpless the spotless-souled

Abdus-Salam must have felt. In his judgment, everything was paradoxical, riddled with contradictions. For instance, the assemblage of teachers with whom he had association customarily exhorted the virtues of reading and learning but was itself starkly ignorant with no inclination towards reading whatsoever. Around him, the ones enveloped in the drapery of religion, proselytizing their faith incessantly, were nothing but partisans to tyrants, rogues and the affluent. The indigent folks of the Left who incited rallies and strikes every now and then in the name of the betterment of the masses could be commonly bought or were innocuous and ineffectual. In their midst, it was a challenge for him to preserve the essence of his individuality. In accepting that challenge, and in the exertion to plant himself deep in the depths of society, there was a scatter perhaps, which had crept into his disposition, which he did not understand . . . But one can gain an insight into his state from his writings.

It was Abdus-Salam's observation that those who pray five times a day and invoke Sharia, the Islamic code of conduct, at the slightest pretext, are more often than not avaricious, arrogant, cowardly, ignorant and vainglorious. The spirit of Faith and the sweet sap of spirituality reside far from their conscience. All these ruminations augmented the dejected state of his heart, and a sceptical cynicism, like a lost bird, began to inhabit his soul.

On the other hand, due to an unequivocal state of paradox and contradiction that was evident in the actions, outlook and personal conduct of his acquaintances, irrespective of whoever represented whichever class, Abdus-Salam's faith in humanity had become infirm to a certain degree. He used to wonder: 'Why do people insist on being what they are not?' The overt expression of his inner churning is also apparent in the sentence that he had quoted in his article, 'Man and Human, a primal struggle': 'What is the gain in living in this world where the tongue falsifies whatever the eye sees.' In fact, this quote belongs to the Urdu critic, Varis Alvi, but due to an oversight, he had ascribed it to Varis Ali Shah Baba Surati. It cannot even be asserted with certainty whether he made this error inadvertently, or if some mischief lurked in its shadows.

The conflicting travails of life had made Abdus-Salam bitter, and due to this, he found himself shackled to a peculiar feeling of loss.

Some people revealed that in his youth he was prone to quarrelling with people. Dissecting their duplicity and untrue proclamations, he thrust the double-faced character of their personas in their faces. But soon enough, he realized that if he kept walking the same thorny path, the day would not be far when he would find himself isolated; when people would call him a lunatic, a loony and a rabble-rouser. It was also possible that some would label him sacrilegious and errant. In this society, the most efficient weapon for persecuting and isolating someone is to label the person sacrilegious, 'without religion'. Undoubtedly, people have flaunted an inborn proficiency in deploying this weapon.

The world from which he had come:

His two friends from childhood, Rafiq and Shafiq, had neared insanity due to dire financial conditions and mental stress. Usually, they never spoke to anyone, but constantly created an uproar, hurled relentless expletives and broke things. They blatantly cursed not only the God of Muslims but the gods of all the world's religions. Once in a while, when Abdus-Salam visited them, people would be astounded as to what got into these two madmen that they sat in total silence in his presence. He would talk to them with profound empathy. Fixing their gazes on a distant void, they would keep listening to him. When someone had wanted to know from Abdus-Salam the mystery of this behaviour, he had spontaneously emitted this sentence: 'I merely divulge to them the inventory of all others with whom God has been unjust.'

The curious person who had asked the question remained silent. Abdus-Salam knew the reason for his silence. He thus expanded further: 'Hearing my words, maybe they feel their sorrows lessened, and their mental imbalance redundant. Maybe they consider me crazy, and thus, turn silent. No?'

The person who had asked the question smiled and left.

Abdus-Salam lifted his eyes to the sky and said: 'What insanity is this, yaar? Can't you control it?' But instantly, he remembered Nietzsche's remark that God had created ninety per cent of people as imbeciles so that His dominion over them would remain perpetual, His worshippers would be in the majority.

Yet, Abdus-Salam had begun to sense that the Almighty had handed the reins of the world to those very ten per cent of people who had no great attachment to the Almighty! Those ten per cent of individuals had taken the leftover ninety per cent of humankind hostage, all in the name of God. When this thought had first sprouted in his mind, he had muttered with a smile: 'Yaar . . . who are You with? The ones who are with You, perhaps You are not with them. The ones who are not with You but just claim to be with You . . . You are frequently seen with them. Your impartiality, too, is cast into suspicion. It doesn't take You a fraction to change parties. You were with Abu Sufyan in Mecca. In Karbala, You allied with Yazid. In Germany, Hitler too, You supported fervently. Since quite a few years now, Your blessings seem to be raining on America, the murderer of innocent citizens of Afghanistan and Iraq. Your record is patently dismal; assessing it, it seems that You only consort with power and the powerful . . . isn't it?'

Ha ha ha ha ha . . .

After some moments, he said slowly: 'If You existed, You wouldn't be so partisan. Perhaps You don't exist! Isn't it, You?'

Rafiq's insanity kept rising with the passage of time. His elder sister was married into a business family in a different state, but her marriage was barely three months old when a natural calamity burst upon the state. Local Muslims revealed that a torrent of bloody rain accompanied by heart-rending lashes of lightning was unleashed during the darkest hours of the night, which the authorities brushed under the carpet saying that in fact, it was nothing but heavy snow. Whosoever claimed to have seen the rain of blood would be treated in a mental asylum. These asylums, a collaboration between the government and 'PHP Company of Colourless Heart', were created recently for the treatment of Muslims, where policemen were employed as doctors. Several regions of the state received bloody rain, but looking at the images that the media broadcast under the directives of the government, it seemed as if the weather couldn't be better, with a veil of mist enveloping the city in its embrace. But the local inhabitants disclosed later to their kin that at first, there would be a downpour of bloody rain, and then suddenly, random houses would catch fire where at first, their residents would be charred to ashes, and later, all their material possessions, flying in air, would get transferred to the residences of the agents and volunteers of the authorities. Then, flames would consume the houses in their entirety. Houses would keep burning. Screams would forget how to emerge from the throats of people being cooked in the flames and would incarcerate themselves in the recesses of their hearts.

It was during one such bloodthirsty night that Rafiq's sister and her husband were torched to ashes.

In the wake of these suddenly but systematically erupting fires, the government later issued a statement that the purpose of the stringent measures deployed to teach a fitting lesson to the rioters was to ensure lasting peace. In order to establish lasting peace, the indispensable measures that the government takes many a times come with collateral damage. When the news of his sister's death reached Rafiq, he was shrouded with immutable silence. For three days, he kept staring mutely at the sky. On the fourth day, everyone felt as if he was searching for something in the sky but that day, his tormented soul had bid adieu to the world.

Shafiq, however, was cured completely with sustained medical treatment over four to five years. I met him just once. I desired to learn more about Abdus-Salam's life from him. At first, he refused to say anything. But when I informed him that I was planning to publish several books penned by him and was in the midst of writing an extensive article on his life so that people were able to understand the hidden meanings in his writings, he revealed some important things to me. After that communication, my curiosity about Abdus-Salam's life increased manifold. I began to delve into his writings with renewed attention. I sojourned to the places that were mentioned in his diaries and met with a number of people in order to fathom the myriad dimensions of his persona . . . so that a possibility could arise to attempt an exegesis of the hair-splitting exactitude, the esoteric gestures and the dense ambiguities that adorned his pithy lines as well as his expansive writings.

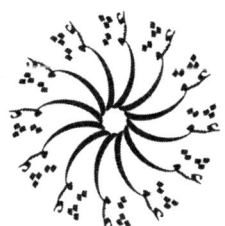

Some of his manifestly illogical notions:

Abdus-Salam used to express eccentric notions about the history of India.

In conversation with friends, or in class sessions in the midst of a lecture, Abdus-Salam, from time to time, offered bewildering and untraditional views about India's history. For instance, his students were once reciting Allama Iqbal's 'Saare Jahaan Se Achcha Hindustan Hamara' (our Hindustan is the best in the whole world). A student inquired: 'Sir, is it true that Greece, Egypt and Rome have perished?'

Abdus-Salam's face turned red. Centring his eyes on the student who had asked the question, he replied: '*Beta*!

Iqbal Sahib was adept at spinning yarns of idiocy. He was not as great an *allama* (knowledgeable) as he is hyped to be. His identity is nothing but hyperbole. In fact, if the anathema of hyperbole is purged from Urdu poetry, all that will survive is rouge-blush, tresses and coquettish glances. The civilizations of Greece, Egypt and Rome, if not greater than Indian civilization, were not less either . . . Allama Iqbal's poetry . . . or any other poet . . . in political discourse or in filmy dialogue . . . never ever trust whatever is peddled about this country. In this country, without any research . . . without perceptive probing . . . sentimental inanities are fabricated. In fact, in matters of history, lies are fabricated . . . So one must think a little before raising questions.'

The students (especially when Abdus-Salam became a tad emotional) would listen to him with undivided attention.

Uninterruptedly for ten minutes, he expressed his thoughts on the above issue. His parting statements, which a student committed to his notebook, were these: 'Civilizations are history. History is beyond amendments. Whatever transpired, transpired. For whatever that transpired, an exploration into whether it transpired in the way in which it has been presented is possible.'

I have already mentioned this fact to you that occasionally, an abstruseness pervaded his speaking, and his interlocutors were deprived of reaching any clear conclusions. But his students had become accustomed to his ambiguous talks. Often, in the classroom, he would employ words that were difficult, and most students struggled to grasp their meaning. Because the students adored him and accorded to his outpourings the raised station of the talk of an intellectual, they had figured out a solution to this quandary. On the following day, the class monitor, after having consulted a dictionary, would come prepared with the meanings of those words and write them down on the board; in the process, there would be quite a bit of clamour in the class. This clamour was primarily due to the reason that the class monitor, who acknowledged Abdus-Salam as his spiritual mentor, would try to explicate again the meanings already elucidated by his teacher. All this would transpire in the free period. The frequent free periods were due to the fact that there were a good number of female teachers in the school who would usually remain absent from the classes during the 'period'. One of the students nonchalantly mentioned an occurrence where Abdus-Salam was in conversation with his students regarding the art of drama. Due to the unstructured progression of his thoughts, the students were unable to understand what he was trying to communicate. At long last, a student mustered the courage to tell him: 'Sir, I do not understand.'

He stopped. Smiled. Then he said: 'Even I do not understand!'

For a few moments, he kept staring at something in space, and then quipped: 'Such conditions too are drama!'

All the students were in splits.

Salam closed the book and listened to the jocular banter from the students. A minute before the ringing of the bell announcing the end of the class, he addressed the students again and said: 'Remember, merely jokes are not drama.' Saying this, he promptly exited the classroom. The monitor stood up to control the class. Instead of listing the roll numbers of the impish, mischievous students on the blackboard, he wrote: 'All that is happening is a joke, and the school in which we are is a joke too.' The entire class burst out laughing; the racket vaulted the walls of the classroom and reached the staffroom, from where it rolled forth into the principal's office. A couple of women-teachers who were cleaning their tiffin boxes dashed to the class on hearing the racket. But their voices of admonition were drowned in the deluge of the students' merry uproar. At long last, the principal came to probe the reason for the students' incessant guffaws that even six teachers were not successful in settling down to silence, and standing outside the classroom, were themselves chuckling at their own incompetency.

But by then, all the students had quietened.

Had they gained the insight that 'this too is a joke?' What other meanings were buried in this phrase? How much pain and how many ecstasies of their existence were cloaked in this phrase? Can pain and ecstasy ever be elucidated?

The principal was endowed with a 'poetic' disposition, but his hold over the students was firm. Whenever he wanted to exact retribution from a particular class, he would unleash ghazals from his unpublished collection of poems in that class for two to three hours. There was a distinct possibility that at his appearance, the students had turned silent with trepidation that they would be subjected to the greatest poetry on earth. Students from the classes in which the principal had recited his verses had reported that before embarking upon his recitation the principal made certain to apprise the gathering that a certain well-educated man (whose name he reveals as Babar Mehdi) had once told him decisively that his poetry stood with the greatest world-poetry. When a student in the grade in which Abdus-Salam was the class teacher told him about this, he had derisively replied that in fact, Babar Mehdi, in the Uzbek language, is a bird that frequently perches on donkeys' backs but donkeys do not feel its presence. The student had understood what Abdus-Salam was hinting at and had laughed for a long time. He never revealed to anyone the principal's worthlessness in Salam's eyes.

His house and his heart:

Abdus-Salam resided in a seven-storey building in Chaar
Bangla (Andheri, Mumbai). His apartment was on the ground
floor. On entering the apartment, one would encounter in
the front cabinet five volumes of the Quran (two English
translations, two Urdu translations and one in the original
Arabic), Urdu-Hindi copies of sermonizing textbooks
Tablighi Nisaab, *Bahishti Zevar* (Paradisiacal Ornaments),
Tarikh e-Anbiya (History of the Prophets), three volumes of
abridged Sha'afi jurisprudence (*Fiqah*), prescribed prayers
(*Masnoon Duaen*), copies of *Khilafat-o-Mulukiyat* and *Pardah*
by the pioneer of Jama'at e-Islami, Maulana Maududi, and
several other canonical religious books. A Persian carpet was

spread on the floor, and there was a fine sofa. On the wall, there was a Sony flat-screen TV, beneath which was a DVD player of a company called Onida. The DVD player was covered with a fine veil imprinted with flowers and petals. An Islamic Hijri calendar as well as a pale-coloured clock were suspended on the wall. On the other wall, there was a sizable frame, which enclosed a velvet background on which the embroidered Quranic verses exhibited an exceptionally refined exemplar of Arabic calligraphy. And the floor was finished with attractive tilework.

Contiguous to the bedroom, there was a small room in which only his long-standing, close friends were permitted. On the door of this special room was inscribed in English: *Dead People's Conference Room*. Only those who had access to this room would know that the room was as convoluted as Abdus-Salam's heart. Everywhere in the room there were heaps of books and files. You could chance upon a representative selection of Urdu and English literature. On the wall was stuck a piece of paper on which writing in blue ink proclaimed: 'Books are the lamentation of the living dead. Come! Let's learn the etiquette of weeping from them.' Then there was this scribbled on the wall with a pencil: 'Truth, in fact, is falsehood.' There were two flowerpots next to the window in this room. There was a money plant in one while the other was filled with some wild grass. Abdus-Salam claimed that there was a unique relationship between the two. No one could comprehend what relationship was possible between a money plant and wild grass. If anyone wanted to know, his ready answer was: 'Contemplate a little. You will figure it out.' But who had the spare time to meditate on such matters! One day, all his friends insisted that he explicate to them what and what kind of relationship he discerned between a money plant and wild grass. He acceded. He said: 'On the eve of Ramazan Eid, I shall invite you all for a meal. I shall tell you then.'

Some reckoned this was all jest and forgot about it. A couple of friends, however, were full of anticipation.

True to his word, Abdus-Salam remembered his promise. On the day of Eid, he slept until the late hours of the morning. When the sun ascended to high noon, he phoned his friends, extended best wishes for Eid to them, and said: 'Come! You want to know the secret of the relationship between the money plant and wild grass, don't you?'

Those who had no other engagements reached his apartment. After the customary greetings, everyone indulged in small talk for some time, and then, Abdus-Salam said: 'Now hear, what is the relationship between the money plant and wild grass.'

Everyone pressed him to reveal the mystery quickly.

'There is only one relationship,' he replied, smiling.

'What?' Everyone pressed him with wonder.

Abdus-Salam kept looking at them silently.

His friends were beginning to suspect that he was going to fool them.

Glancing at their waning faces, he declared: 'Both are appearances of earth; one is a symbol of wealth for us, while the other, a symbol of futility . . . or we could say, of being meaningless.' His friends were staring at his face. He proceeded to explicate further: 'Until the significance of both these is not uniform in your hearts, God shall be unfathomable to your comprehension, and for this very reason, you shall always be in need of an appointed day to be exultant and festive, such as the day of Eid . . .'

His friends were crestfallen at his last sentence. In order to dispel the feeling of dejection, they aimlessly began to look here and there.

Seeing their withered faces, he said: 'Every day is Eid for me. No day is greater or lesser than the other.'

At this pronouncement, however, the silence that had crept in unexpectedly turned even more dense. Abdus-Salam sensed the soiled gravity of the atmosphere. Instantly, with an intention to transform the unexpected grave silence into cheerful congeniality, he declared: 'The biryani has been ordered from Delhi Darbar . . . You all have become so serious. At least on the day of Eid, smile! Come, let's have biryani.'

His friends, trying to produce smiles on their lips, proceeded to the dining hall. Abdus-Salam then murmured silently in his heart: 'See! Even on the day of Eid, I have managed to make Your believers sad. Why do You promise them unreal happiness? It is because of such deeds of Yours that they are not able to inculcate the habit of being naturally happy.' He has mentioned the occurrences of this day in his personal diary. He desired that people would not await a special day to feel happy but become habituated to finding enjoyment in their everyday lives so there would be a growth in their abilities to face the difficulties and severities of life.

His room, apart from the two flowerpots, contained a chest in which there were old pens that had retreated into disuse. But Abdus-Salam was in some way devotedly attached to these old, unused pens. He used to say: 'When a person becomes inept at transcribing his thoughts on paper, pens, fulfilling their duty, inscribe fresh thoughts on their own. Some pens alleged to be without a soul are, in fact, far more intelligent and sensitive than the litterateur. Therefore, they should not be discarded, reckoning them lifeless.' Among the files next to the pen-case was an extremely special file that absolutely no one was permitted to touch in his lifetime. He himself opened it rarely. Whatever it contained was so personal and precious that it could not be shared with anyone at all . . . as if it was the ultimate concealed section of his heart in which the most indescribable memories of his being were safeguarded. Each person has such a secret corner in their heart, as if it is that fundamental centre around which the enigmas of one's individuality keep twirling. Sometimes, in the solitude of the night, when a nameless deluge rushed into the barrenness of Abdus-Salam's heart and each moment became ephemeral and that ephemeral moment's emptiness, becoming a surging stillness, cast the darkness of death over his heart, he would fidget and open the file in the hush of the night and the dreadful darkness of the room. He would then clasp a decrepit photo removed from the sheaf of papers in his hands. Holding back tears, he would press the photo to his chest. And then, for a long time, he would let his tears flow freely in seclusion. In his entire life, he passed through this state twenty-three times. Perhaps it was the photo of that girl whose story he could not put to words in his 'Saga of Passion'. Whenever he passed through this oscillating murky state, the next day, he inscribed in red ink the following couplet in his personal diary:

Kab tak rahega rooh pe pairaahen-e-badan
Kab tak hawaa aseer rahegi hubaab mein

(Till when shall the garment of the body cloak the soul
Till when shall air be captive in a water-bubble)

It took me a long time to arrive at the conclusion that this photo must be of that very girl.

Whenever he has jotted down this couplet, he has numbered it, which totals to twenty-three. But merely by looking at these numbers, it would be inappropriate to establish their relationship with the melancholy of his soul. When I studied the third manuscript of 'Saga of Passion', the mystery of this couplet and the numbers beneath it unravelled for me from the sixth paragraph onwards. He has written that there was one such love too whose memories were rooted in his chest like an arrow. Now and then when those memories tossed and turned in his heart, it seemed as if there was no other cure for this agony except death. In the same paragraph, he has written further that whenever he is in this unbearable state he fervently recalls a couplet of Shakeb Jalali, and his fingers instinctively transcribe that couplet in his diary. Along with transcribing the couplet, he would record the day and date. A possible explanation for this could be that he wanted to remember each time he was steeped in this shattering state when his heart had attempted to draw him to suicide. He has, at one place in his writing, referred to this shattering state as 'the state of living-dying', and I have tried to copy it. But I must confess here that I could not fathom what he meant by this term. Maybe some amongst you may comprehend it.

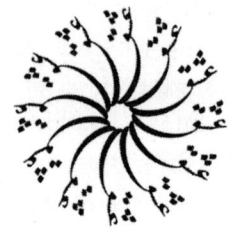

His friends told me that he tried to keep his apartment in an orderly manner. New curtains, new paintings, new glasses, fine doormats, attractive fragrances were all resonant with his temperament, but sometimes, he dawdled considerably before changing and refurbishing even small things. For instance, at someone's suggestion, he bought a peephole for the door, and decided that he would fit it on the door himself. He affixed the peephole in real haste, then went away to the school. Just as he was beginning to settle down after his return in the evening, there was an unexpected knock on the door. As he proceeded to open the door, it occurred to him to look through the peephole to see who was calling on him at this hour. But nothing was visible to him. He was perplexed. He peeked into the peephole again. He could not see anything except darkness. He murmured under his breath: 'Is it God on the other side?'

There were two-three knocks again. He opened the door to find one of his friends there.

The friend was laughing.

'Why are you laughing, yaar?' he enquired.

'What happened?' he asked again.

Giggling away, the friend said· 'First tell me, who has fitted this peephole? I could see your eye from outside.'

Abdus-Salam exclaimed: 'What?' Then he stepped outside and peeked into the peephole. He could see his room slightly larger and wider than it was. He began to smirk at his own folly.

Several days passed but he turned oblivious to rectifying the position of the peephole. If anyone questioned him about it, he would reply: 'I believe in transparency.'

Increasingly, his visitors became accustomed to peering into the room through the peephole before knocking. He too was aware of this; he would ruminate: 'God, You have done one good thing, namely the proclamation that You are going to address everyone along with their mothers' names on the Day of Judgement. Otherwise, these ill-fated ones would have been so dejected . . .' Once, he had grinned at this thought, but later he mused: 'I envy God's intellect. Maybe He exists and smiles too.' Then raising his eyes to the sky, he winked and said: 'You know, don't You . . . what my relation is to the children of Hameeda Syed and Kulsum Pathan from the old building?' Pressing his fingers to his lips then, he tossed a flying kiss towards the heavens for the Almighty.

Astute reader! If I include this episode in the novel, do not ask me whether that kiss reached the Almighty, or whether the angels intercepted it somewhere in the firmament, cut it and pasted it in the 'register of reckoning'.

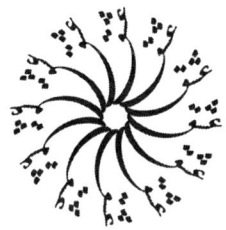

A friend of his once asked him: 'The religious books that you have in the glass bookcase in the drawing room, why don't you have such books in your study?' Placing his hand on the friend's shoulder, Abdus-Salam said: 'The fact of the matter is that when religious books are kept with books of literature, they begin to proselytize. They start accusing some books of obscenity, of distracting thoughts and emotions, or of offending virtuous morality. It degenerates into a brawl, yaar . . . Visibly . . . these books are cover-bound but when they become angry, they begin to threaten the use of abusive language, violence, murder intrigues and social boycott. My heart sinks. I have, thus, set them apart, and kept them in this room in front of everybody.'

The friend, shaking his head incredulously, was trying to grasp what Abdus–Salam was saying.

Abdus–Salam then concluded: 'You see, by setting them apart . . . they get attention from the visitors to the house. The moment they get some attention, their aggression cools down, and the visitors, finding them in my drawing room, consider me devout. And they too are contented.'

'In other words, you are indulging in tomfoolery with others.'

'No, what is the need for that?'

(Both smile.)

'The truth is that the beauty of existence is veiled in its contradictions. A host of dead books have become an expedient way of retaining the relationships of living people.'

The friend concurred and said: 'You sometimes speak truly "solid" Urdu.'

Ushering the conversation on further: 'There is one more advantage to the books in this bookcase. Due to their presence, people tolerate my utterances. Their presence in the house is a sign to others that "he is one of us". Otherwise, yaar, you know very well . . . In any case, who really comprehends these books?'

'You have a point. These days, I too am detecting that it is under the pretext of all this that maulana *log* are sowing discord amongst Muslims,' the friend said before the end of the conversation. He was the one who had been expelled from a mosque three or four months ago with the excuse that Wahabis were not permitted to pray in that mosque.

(A few questions:)

Are individuals like Abdus-Salam scarce in our society?

Are individuals like Abdus-Salam created by God, or are they culpable in creating themselves? If these characters are misfits in society, is society responsible for it or God? Can God fit in a society in which Abdus-Salam is at ease?

In the wake of my desire to present Abdus-Salam as a character in a novel, I began to pass through an odd creative difficulty. The issue is, as a novelist, will all responsibility for crafting Abdus-Salam's character be enforced upon me? Shall I be accountable for all his actions? I have also been prey to the misgiving as to how shall his own selfhood and persona present itself in the novel without my authorial will?

How shall he remain captive in the creative world shaped by me after all the knowledge I have amassed about his life? In addition to these questions, some other much more imperative questions distress me due to being a novelist who was born in India. For instance, if the acts of individuals are unethical, is it errant to describe them as they are? How should individuals' distant from religion be described? If a person spews obscenities in day-to-day life, should the writer expunge him? If a character reminisces about his past loves and sexual relations with an amplified emotional attachment in some exceptional state, should they not be revealed? If a character throws into question societal norms, religion and morality, should they not be deliberated upon just because a sizable number among the readers here are intransigently religious? Before embarking upon writing, should a writer ask religious leaders how much freedom he has to portray the stark realities of life? Is literature's task to tutor people how to lead their lives, or to reveal to them how irretrievably folks are mired in the quicksand of life? Is literature a counsellor, or originator of uninhibited narrative that presents a reflection of progressing life in the text?

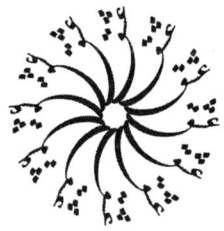

A litterateur is frequently face-to-face with these and many other questions of the kind, but there are some other questions too that surface in my mind. For example, is the classical form of the novel still relevant? The form bound to opening . . . ascension . . . epilogue. Is the account of the character's birth, youth and fate, or the character's mental states, important? How can one step outside the flow of cognizance? Is experimenting with form appropriate for all novels? Without being familiar with the stylistic modes of the novel at the stratum of art, are there possibilities of contribution in this domain? Is repeating the form indicative of a dearth of creative vigour? Is it fair to compare the artistic approach of novelists such as Gustave Flaubert,

Victor Hugo, Leo Tolstoy, Gabriel Garcia Marquez and Milan Kundera to that of Indian and Urdu novelists? Is the mandate of a novelist in this rapidly changing world to uphold a singular linguistic and religious culture, or to attain insightful knowledge of collective consciousness? Entangled in the Western and Eastern exegeses of gnosis on a cultural stratum, should one venerate religious bonds, or embrace the path to broadmindedness? Why is the Indian and especially the Urdu milieu so withdrawn from prose and creative writing?

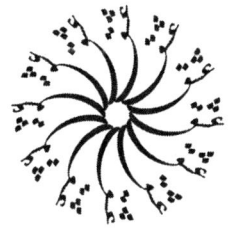

These questions kept churning in my mind even while delving into the material collected with the purpose of writing a novel about Abdus-Salam's life, while reading his diaries as well as other articles. This was also because Abdus-Salam himself was an avid reader and writer, and fancied himself a novelist. Even though he was an English teacher, his bond with Urdu literature was rooted firm. A couple of times, I was amazed by how alike his thoughts about fiction were to mine. He says: 'Life is akin to water, wind and fragrance who have no form, no shape, no visage. A novel too should be like life.' And I adore his famed proclamation: 'Novel is God's criticism on life . . . Such a

God who exists but is nowhere present.' I always feel that
I wanted to write this sentence.

While sketching the outline of the novel based on
Abdus-Salam's character, I have related some apprehensions
of my heart to you. I can inscribe these ruminations in this
outline, but in the novel, it will be considered a flaw. Many a
times, this thought too occurred to me that writing a novel
will not be easy just on the basis of secondary information.
My acquaintance with the aesthetics of the novel is still
poor. Therefore, there is a likelihood of errors and lapses.
It is quite probable that while writing, I might go astray in
several places. On a different note, one writing of Abdus-
Salam's impressed me substantially. He has written that the
novel is beauty. A beautiful thing, due to its unity, finish and
make, appears attractive to every viewer. No one needs an
explanation of why that particular thing is beautiful. If we
feel the need to explicate to someone the reason for such
and such a thing being beautiful, then it is an argument for
a want of beauty in that particular thing. A novel should
be precisely like that. The minute the beauty of a novel
becomes reliant on someone's interpretation, it will be
deemed as a want of beauty in the novel.

While gathering information about his life, I wondered
several times, what kind of life is this whose essence is
dependent on paradox? Can we lead a life that is, from the
beginning, decreed as determined, appropriate, rehearsed
and perfect? Abdus-Salam's declaration in this context is
significant, that we have been handed this mandate of living
without making us rehearse for it.

I am thinking, how shall I compose in the classical form
of the novel the story of a man in whose life there was

nothing but disintegration. There was never ever a balance in his deeds . . . whose life was disordered, non-intentional, like a rolling wave.

Will a novel based on such an existence rise to the expectations of the aesthetics of beauty?

A night's account:

At a journey of around two to two-and-a-half hours from Mumbai, there is a region called Kasara. It is a mountainous terrain as far as the eye can see. Looking down from the tops of the hills, a couple of sad rivers can be seen crawling and twisting away. During the rainy season, when the gathering dark clouds pour their hearts out over this mountainous region, the rivers flow with dark earthy red and white foam. But even then, it feels as if the song of a woman barred and fated for separation has permeated the atmosphere of Kasara ghat. If the Urdu poet Rajinder Manchanda Bani had sojourned to this place, then in view of the heart-rending sadness of this mountainous terrain, he would have addressed it as an 'absurd commentary on the environs of being'. However, Abdus-Salam has written favourably about Kasara, saying that seeing the spread of mountains there had served to alleviate his loneliness. If one were to enter into a discourse with the vistas of nature here, one would receive unexpected answers from the other side of the wall of silence. The flowing sadness permeating the atmosphere converses with the sadness of the heart due to which there is a decrease in the loneliness of being.

To the south of Kasara is a little village named 'Dil Muztarabad', which is flanked by high mountains. A friend of Abdus-Salam's, Sarfaraz Subedar, was born in this village. Sarfaraz was a lecturer in psychology at a college in Mumbai. Whenever they found the time, both of them would go away to 'Dil Muztarabad'. Abdus-Salam spent some of the saddest evenings of his life in this village. In winters here, the sun turns into a yellow flower with the advent of the evening. After some time, it is seen floating in a lake smeared with fog. Progressively, the fog begins to absorb the colours of the yellow flower, and then, the moment arrives when the eye sees that the yellow flower, wilting away, perishes in the frosty lake smeared with sad mist. This scene, each time, would deepen his loneliness for a while.

That day too, the halo of the yellow flower had scattered over the lake smeared with sad mist. Who knows which mourning's initiation it was, for Abdus-Salam's heart had been snuffed since dusk. A pointed insight was lost somewhere in his heart, and his mind was going in circles around that insight. Who knows what wounds have long been wedged in our hearts; we imagine that the wound has healed and its scar has vanished but that is not the case. Due to the searing heat of a distinctive moment, these wounds open up again. They rise as dust-clouds from the ruins of the past inhabiting the heart, and in an imperceptible way, begin to consume the soul. They begin to wander in the eyes and become the reason for an intense internal anguish.

The pale-hued fog was not successful in bestowing a new colour to Abdus-Salam's face; it is probably for this reason that he too was brimming with melancholy.

When the mist weeps a lot in the night, the windows of the houses in 'Dil Muztarabad' are coated with a patina of its tears, on which children can be seen engrossed in writing Marathi alphabets *a, aa, ii* . . . That night too, the icy loneliness was not some natural occurrence; in fact, the grief-laden dilemmas in the maze of Abdus-Salam's heart too had a role to play in it. A gnawing sense of purposeless, of a futile life without destination, had shaped its partial, incomplete visage somewhere deep inside, which he had been successful in incarcerating in the dungeon of his inner self to uphold social relations . . . but he was in perpetual conflict due to the distress and discontent born out of that contradiction. In this conflict-laden, stormy distress and discontent, the lamentation for his soul, which had been severed from God, was in progress too.

The night's long shadow had spread over wild bushes and trees.

The buzz of insects surged from the stubs of dry grass, bushes and branches of half-drowsy trees, and was intoxicating enough to carry the winds far away with it. Abdus-Salam saw darkness as brightness. Due to the darkness in this forest, the sightless birds snoozing in his heart writhed and fluttered. He saw: the sightless birds emerge out of the secret chamber of his heart and begin to glow like fireflies around him in the dark of the night.

Where do fireflies come from?

From where does Man come on this earth?

Why does God exist?

Is soul a firefly?

Is the firefly God?

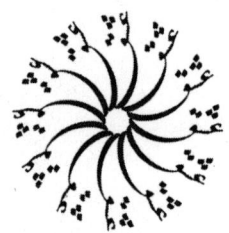

Questions would spring in Abdus-Salam's mind as if he were a vortex, and these questions revolutions of the self in which his soul was plunging.

In those moments, he was perhaps thinking that if God was a spirit, and if he had bound Him in his heart's secret chamber, then what meaning did the arduous path of prayers and devotion have? Could it be that prayers were instruments, weapons or a conspiracy to keep individuals far away from political matters and make them submissive to the state? Did the religious preachers who had attained power on the basis of doctrinal beliefs keep utilizing the gullibility of the masses as a shield for their political gains?

Sarfaraz, seated a little distance away, was smoking a cigarette. He knew that when Abdus-Salam was silent, he should not be disturbed.

Perhaps Abdus-Salam perceived God as Truth, which can be fathomed neither by a collective eye nor by a succession of prayers. 'Each individual, each soul is an exclusive experience, and each individual, each soul's relationship with God will be shaped by the levels of its sagacity and insight. God is formless, without past, beyond desire, omnipresent, and without future, eternal. Man is bound to the past, desires, place and time. Both are each other's need, and each other's creation.' He had transcribed these lines in his personal diary a few days after an excursion to 'Dil Muztarabad'.

Abdus-Salam lit his cigarette with Sarfaraz's cigarette . . . and then was immersed in thought. He thought:

The relationship that exists between God and Man can be experienced on the singular summit of cognition after which one is able to gain a profound insight into life's transformations; an insight due to which the true reality of silence, smile and love becomes visible to Man. He took a long drag of the cigarette, and then thought: through the gnosis of self, life, turning into an experiential truth, becomes pleasurable.

The smoke of the cigarette spread within Abdus-Salam's chest, and with his breath, a number of sightless birds, freed from the captivity of centuries, spread in the solitude of the dark night . . . now they were spreading radiance in the surrounding blackness.

For a long spell, silence cast its shadow over 'Dil Muztarabad'.

Both had smoked numerous cigarettes.

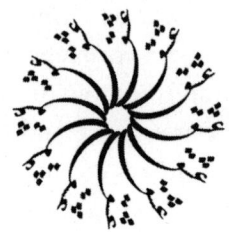

'What is the matter, Abdus-Salam? You seem very dejected,'
Sarfaraz said.

'Yaar, endless thoughts overrun my heart.'

'What thoughts?'

(An interval)

'What thoughts, yaar?'

'Who are we, yaar, who are watching these mountains?
Are we, too, merely a spectacle for someone who is watching
us from afar? And we are nothing but a spectacle . . .'

'You too, yaar . . . what all do you keep thinking about!'

'What can I do, yaar . . . these thoughts make me restless.'

'Why do you unnecessarily torment your brain? Here,
have some maava.'

'Which one is it?'

'I know, yaar . . . the one you consume . . . the same, Bhola, katri supari, star mar kar . . .'

A faint smile spread on Abdus-Salam's lips. Sarfaraz handed the maava to him.

Both of them sat there for some time. Savouring the maava, the dusty fog in Abdus-Salam's heart had dissipated.

When they returned, Sarfaraz's mother prepared tea for them. Seated in the house, they began to sip their tea. Outside, the world of fireflies too became extinct. A world that was never there; it was merely Abdus-Salam's illusion.

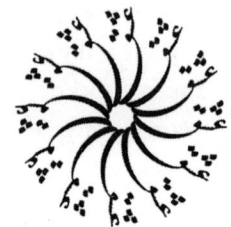

A strange experience in his life:

Abdus-Salam's maternal cousin (his mother's sister's daughter) was older than him. Abdus-Salam had attended her wedding along with his parents. The wedding took place in his ancestral village, which was located roughly seven-and-a-half hours away from Mumbai. He had thoroughly enjoyed the village wedding. He was not too accustomed to Konkani customs and the dialect; despite that, he found the environs there to his liking. Three days after returning to Mumbai, his aunt called up and informed his mother that Shagufta had quit her in-law's house and returned home. She was not willing to stay with her husband; she wanted a divorce.

Abdus-Salam's parents were quite distressed by this news. Throughout the day, they conferred with other relatives. When Abdus-Salam became aware of this matter after his return from college, he was astonished at first, but then, the complexity of the situation piqued his interest. He wanted to fathom the riddle of what would drive a girl to insist on divorce merely two or three days after being married. Therefore, when his father voiced his intention of leaving for the village, Abdus-Salam declared that he too would join him.

A few elders of the village were seated in the courtyard; close relatives were settled in the house.

Shagufta was seated in a room with mud walls. A forty-watt bulb was on in the room; stray bugs and insects were swirling around its pale light. A lamp, its flame flickering, was in an alcove, and the holy book was placed across from it. This book was read and consulted solely in the month of Ramazan, and all oaths were bound to it. In one corner, there was a quilt spread over a mat. If one saw the quilt during the daytime in proper brightness, then one would appreciate the amazing skill and artisanship that had gone into its making. Such striking floral motifs, birds and geometric patterns were woven into it! Then there was a spittoon placed on one side, and next to it, paan, a pouch with *supari* (betel nuts) and a nutcracker. Along with these was a small copper pot filled with water. The floor was smoothened with dung. Lastly, the walls of the room were coated with brownish-red mud.

Everyone had tried to persuade Shagufta to reconsider, but she was unwavering in her decision. Her family members had spoken to her husband's family; they were amenable to making compromises. But Shagufta was adamant on getting a divorce. She kept saying that if she could not get a divorce, she would give precedence to death.

Listening to the elders seated in the courtyard, Abdus-Salam could not arrive at an equitable conclusion; in fact, the knot was ravelling more and more. He thought, he would personally meet Shagufta and her mother and try to gain some understanding of the problem.

After knocking on the door with the doorknocker, he entered the dimly lit room in which slivers of moonlight entered through the cracks between the walls. Shagufta was seated in the corner, her back supported by the wall, her arms wrapped around her knees.

'*Bhana* (sister).'

'Who is it?'

'I, Abdus-Salam, from Mumbai.'

'*Arre*, come, sit.'

She released her arms from around her knees and made space for him on the quilt.

Abdus-Salam deposited himself close to her. He had never seen Shagufta's face at such proximity before. Her bright eyes were centred on Abdus-Salam. There was a kind of forbearance in her eyes, which he had never noticed earlier.

'Why have you come?'

'I felt bad.'

'Everyone is feeling bad.'

'But why, *aapa*?'

'You are still young . . . one has to be a grown-up to understand these things,' Shagufta replied in a remarkably even tone.

'Aapa, I am a grown-up.'

'Silly; not a grown-up like that. You should have some experience of life.'

'I have a lot.'

A smile blossomed on Shagufta's face.

'Bhana, I want to know. Do you not like the guy?'

'No, it is not that.'

'You have an issue with your in-laws?'

'No, they are fine too.'

Slapping his palm on his forehead, Abdus-Salam exclaimed: 'Arre, then what *is* the problem?'

'There are some things, and to understand them, one has to be a grown-up,' Shagufta replied in an explicatory manner this time.

'Do not dupe me by conjuring up evasive answers. Is it that your spouse has rejected you?'

'Absolutely not.'

'Then why . . . Why the entire family . . .'

Abdus-Salam could not finish the sentence. Shagufta had placed her hand over his lips.

Just then, a girl from the neighbourhood entered the room, a tall girl with an ample body who must have been around twenty-four to twenty-five years of age.

'Shagufta, the fish needs to be fried.'

'Okay, you proceed.'

As she was leaving, she paused for a moment and looked at Abdus-Salam. Salam was then at the cusp of adolescence where he was not in a state to understand what pausing and eyeing someone in this manner meant, what undertones it carried.

'Arre, Kulsum, he is my brother.'

This sentence was a bit unanticipated, and Shagufta's tone too was slightly odd to him. For a second, Abdus-Salam felt he was still very small.

The girl with the sharp, chiselled outlines was gone, but the features of her visage rested in Abdus-Salam's eyes for a while, and then were archived in his memory.

'Who was she, aapa?'

'She is my close friend.'

'I see.' Saying this, Abdus-Salam tried to raise his eyes with the intention of looking into Shagufta's bright eyes, but his effort to do so failed him. Instead, his gaze stuck on the forty-watt bulb around which stray bugs and insects were still swirling. From a slit in the wall, a house-lizard was peering at them. Some dead insects were strewn on the floor. What kind of light is this that attracts bugs and insects to itself, and then turns out to be their deathtrap!

Abdus-Salam kept sitting there for a long time, but he did not receive the answer for which he was fishing. After a two-day stay in the village, he returned to Mumbai with his father. A few weeks later, with the intercession of the imam in the village, Shagufta's husband granted her a divorce. For several months, Abdus-Salam was snared in perplexity. Kulsum's sharp features would occupy his memory, and he would feel as if her alluring and luminous eyes were glaring at him. What could be the reason? He would ponder, but would arrive at no clarity.

Six months after Shagufta's divorce, he wrote a letter to her.

Once in a while, he would also enquire about the well-being of his relatives from her.

His college was closed for a week due to the Christmas break. He decided that he would spend his holidays in the village. As much as he wanted to converse with Shagufta, he equally desired to once again gaze at Kulsum's eyes. God knows why he was not able to forget those eyes! He obtained permission from his parents and left for the village.

Had Shagufta's tragedy created some compassion in his heart? Or was it that the sorcery of Kulsum's alluring luminous eyes was seeking a distinct story in his unconscious? Throughout his journey, his chin resting on the sill of the open window of the state transport bus, he absorbed the trees, patches of fields and tiny hamlets. Shagufta's forlorn face veiled in descending dusk had faded somewhere. For a mere fraction, some lone feature of her face would make an appearance and revert to the dusky recesses of his mind.

When he reached the threshold of Shagufta's house, the sun's rays had retreated to its scarlet halo. There was a guava tree in the courtyard, and it was looking a little gloomy. For the past several days, at the advent of evening, a bird with a green tail would fly in and perch on its dry branch and tweet a portion of 'Forgotten Dastan' (tale). The tale was written by someone around 1857. Every day, the bird would end the story at such a tragic turn that the sadness of the tree would intensify further. 'Forgotten Dastan' was very long, and the bird had made a promise to the guava tree that it would not reveal anything about itself until the tale was concluded. The secret was that the bird had escaped from the court of the 'Taus Chaman', the Peacock Garden. The name of its master was Tilism-e-Naiyer, the son of Ganjifa, the son of Itr-e-Kafur.

Contiguous to the door of the courtyard was the room for receiving the guests, known as *vatedaar* in Konkani. From there, a door led to the interior of the house. Inside, there were two rooms, one each on the left and the right. In one of the rooms was a staircase leading to the upper storey. After that, descending a little, there was *padi*, a kitchen space in which there was a bathroom on one side and a stove on the other. Meals were prepared in the padi. In one corner, there was a stack of firewood and dried leaves. There was a door to reach the backyard from the padi. The padi was coated with dung. The outer walls of the courtyard were made of stone. Such walls are called *gadga* in Konkani. Adjoining the gadga were two mango trees bearing alphonso mangoes, and a coconut palm. In one corner was a *khopti* (a small storage hutch) in which branches and twigs to be used for the fire were kept.

He called out from the vatedaar.

Shagufta was in the padi at the time. She merely felt a vibration of sound in her ears and walked towards the vatedaar. On seeing Salam, a smile lit her face. She stepped forward, and taking the suitcase from his hand, enquired: 'Arre, suddenly?'

'Yes, I was missing you.'

'A brother ought to be like you! Come, come in.'

His aunt was in the padi, sifting rice to discard the tiny pebbles in it. Abdus-Salam greeted her. Getting up, she embraced him.

'Have some *alma* (*sulemani* tea, brewed with whole spices, jaggery and lemon).'

'Don't put too much tea.'

Shagufta busied herself with preparing the tea. Abdus-Salam went to the *mangildar* (backyard) to wash and refresh himself. Placing the vessel with tea on the woodstove, Shagufta removed a fresh towel from the *hadpa* (a large wooden storage trunk used to store food items, uncooked grain and other valuable things).

'Looks like it is foreign.'

'Yes,' she turned and replied.

The tea was boiling. Shagufta snuffed out the firewood of the stove. Salam was just done wiping his face with the towel when he spotted Kulsum on the footpath outside the wall of the courtyard. She too was looking at him. In the faint pale glow of the bulb, her face looked even more alluring and enigmatic.

When their eyes met, Kulsum asked: 'When did you arrive?'

'Today . . . just now.'

'I see.'

Then Kulsum said, raising her voice: 'Arre, Shagufta, where are you?'

Shagufta barely managed to prevent the teacup from slipping out of her hands.

'Coming,' Shagufta responded, pushing the teacup into Abdus-Salam's hands.

'Tell me?'

'Tomorrow, I will need your new blouse.'

'You will get it.'

'Okay, then I will talk to you tomorrow.'

Teacup in his hand, Abdus-Salam stood there listening to their exchange.

Kulsum turned to leave. Taking a step forward, she stopped, and turning her head, looked at Shagufta and Abdus-Salam. The glow of the pale-yellow bulb had turned even more yellow. The light steeped in pale yellow had accentuated the gloominess of the guava tree. The wall of the courtyard was hollowed out in places. A snake had been dwelling there for many years. The koyal, perched on the coconut palm, kept musing about its futile soaring through the day. Shagufta centred her gaze on Abdus-Salam, but he did not have the nerve to look into her eyes. He took the last sip of tea and kept staring at the tea leaves settled at the bottom of the cup. The snake lodged in the wall of the courtyard was familiar with the scent of all the people in the house and street. Abdus-Salam's scent was new to it, and thus, it became a bit alert. Otherwise, after sunset, it would have slithered from its hollow and slid through the wild shrubbery behind the wall to the nearby wilderness in pursuit of its prey. This was its habit, but today, a new scent had made it cautious.

Kulsum vanished from his eyes.

But her mysterious eyes, right there, were peering at Abdus-Salam in the pale-yellow glow of the bulb. There was an unsettling emotion of resentment for Abdus-Salam in those eyes, but he was incapable of reading that emotion. It had been quite some time since Kulsum had left, but he felt as if she was present somewhere close, as if she was watching him, in fact, glaring at him . . . but was not visible to him. For some moments, he was riddled with perplexity. For this very reason, a desire ignited in him to know why Kulsum looked at him in such a manner. He considered many possibilities but did not reach a conclusion.

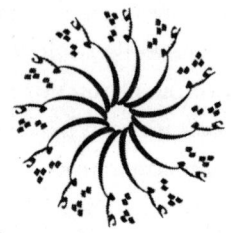

That night, at dinner, conversation revolved around the family and relations. Three of their relatives had passed away in the past months, and they too were remembered. Shagufta informed him that a distant relative, Suleman Karbari, had been bitten by a snake in the field. He was a courageous man. He had spent his entire life farming in the jungles. His fields were right in the midst of a thick forest. It was said that he was familiar with wild animals and all kinds of snakes. He caught the snake that had bitten him and brought it along with him to the village. The venom had spread in his body, but even then, he had gripped the mouth of the snake like a vice. It was a very big snake, approximately twelve to fifteen feet long. Some people rushed to fetch a doctor.

Suleman *mamu* (uncle) was urged to release the snake; someone else would kill it. But he refused, saying that if the snake died, he too would die. It was necessary that it stay alive until the doctor's arrival. On hearing this, everyone desisted from freeing the snake from his hand forcibly. Everyone stood around him quietly. The doctor was delayed; he was on a visit to another village. Suleman mamu's condition began to deteriorate. The imam of the mosque recited a verse from the Quran and blew his breath (for benedictions) over a cup filled with water. Suleman mamu was made to drink that water three times, but there was no improvement. His breathing became heavy and uneven, and the colour of his eyes began to change. Despite this, he did not let go of the snake. Just when the doctor arrived, a youth from the village managed to wrench the snake from his hand, but precisely at that instant, Suleman mamu took his last breath. The youth who had wrenched the snake from mamu's hand informed everyone that the snake too had died.

Abdus-Salam was in a state of wonder for a long time after hearing this episode. He had never seen Suleman Karbari, but the silhouette of a huge, powerful man holding a snake that was writhing in his vice-like grip appeared before his eyes. For a long time, he stared raptly at the powerful silhouette . . . Then the conversation turned to other people and the atmosphere changed. The snake and the colossal silhouette disappeared from his vision.

In the meantime, his aunt brought in a tray of roasted *kolim* (tiny shrimp) and placed it in front of him. The kolim were mixed with chopped onions and green chilies. He tasted a little. He was eating roasted kolim after quite a long time. He relished its flavour. Without realizing it, he polished off half the tray of kolim, and kept praising his aunt's culinary skills. Shagufta quite liked this appreciative manner of his even though it was she who, after cleaning the kolim, had dried and roasted them.

In Konkan, it is a norm to sit in the courtyard after dinner and indulge in a bit of chitchat. The star-filled sky, twinkling away, bears witness to this banter. Salam wondered why such a bright sky was not visible in the metropolis, Mumbai. He kept gazing at the Milky Way. The night scattered all around had its own tongue. The night speaks only in that tongue, and Abdus-Salam had not yet begun to understand it. But he had certainly fathomed this much that the night had its own demeanour, its own tongue and its own stories. It is imperative to shower special attention on the night. It is essential to gaze upon her to one's heart's content. He realized that music issues forth from the branches of mango, peepal and jackfruit trees, music in which a song is submerged. One just has to focus one's ears on it. On one side of the courtyard, some straw had been fumigated from which faint curls of smoke wafted in ripples, and after drifting awhile, were lost in the night's veil. Fumigation is essential to ward off insects and bugs, and to protect oneself from mosquitos.

His aunt was happy and cheerful. She enquired about many things from Abdus-Salam. Revelling in the rustling sounds of the night, he answered her. In between, Shagufta too enquired about his studies and future plans. He too was burning to ask Shagufta a question, but for that, his aunt's absence was indispensable.

Call it a coincidence that his aunt went to the shed to fetch the little box containing paan and betel nut.

'Shagufta aapa, Kulsum seems a little strange.'

Laughing, Shagufta said: 'She is very nice.'

'Yes . . . but there is an unusual fire in her eyes, no?'

'You think so . . . then it must be.'

'Since when have you known her?'

'We are childhood friends . . . She loves me very much.'

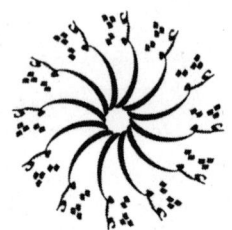

At that time, 'love' was just a plain, unloaded word for Abdus-Salam. To become acquainted with the multiplicity and complexity of this word, perhaps he truly needed to grow up a little more. Had Shagufta forgotten that Abdus-Salam had not yet become that mature!

(One morning, after a few days.)

His aunt made *ghaaone* (a sweet akin to sweet rotis) for him to savour along with his tea, and he ate it with great relish, all the while showering praises on his aunt. After tea, he squatted close to the woodstove and talked about the village with his aunt. After a while, a few relatives dropped by to meet him, and he spent some time with them. After lunch, he lay down, resting. Soon he dozed off. After a while, Kulsum dropped in. She and Shagufta sat chatting in the padi. Then Shagufta, on the pretext of some work, took her to the room within. His aunt had gone to the bush to fetch firewood. It had been half-an-hour since Shagufta and Kulsum had gone to the room.

The resounding silence suffusing the house woke up Abdus-Salam. He peeked in the direction of the padi. The door was locked from the inside. He turned to look at Shagufta's room. That too was shut. Quietly, his feet barely touching the ground, he went to the padi. There was no one there. He then went towards Shagufta's room and stood next to the door.

They both were in deep conversation in the room. From the other side of the earthen wall, their faint voices could be heard . . . The flow of words would abruptly break but would resume after a few seconds. This too was a prime reason for the rise in Abdus-Salam's curiosity. Pressed to the wall, he stood quietly. The wall was confounded by this act of his. After a while, the words ceased to emanate. He felt the silence spreading around him. After ten to twelve minutes, astonishing undulations of temperate breathing, in a flow, suffused the room. Salam sensed the vibrations produced by those undulations. One of his palms was pressed to the wall. The earthen clay of the wall would first absorb the undulations of the sound, and then transfer an indistinct sensation to Abdus-Salam's palm. It seemed as if within these vibrations there was an intensity and warmth, but the passion of this enchanting vibration did not want to reveal itself to Abdus-Salam. However, when the succession of hazy impressions of the sound's undulations ended, he heard one sentence of Shagufta's with abundant clarity.

'Not today. My brother is here. He will wake up.'

On hearing this, Abdus-Salam, soft-footedly, returned to his bed and lay down.

The impression, which had been transported to his soul from the earthen wall, enclosed a covert sign that unravelled the enigma of Shagufta's divorce for him. For a long while, he reflected on the connotations of covert signs. He kept thinking about those vibrations in which he had sensed the possibility of a fusion of warm intensity. He focused on the sentence that would always reside in his memory. He remembered those eyes; Kulsum's eyes that glared at him as if he was some calamity, a rival, a disagreeable person. He kept brooding . . . for a day, two days, three days, ten days, several days, several months . . . Whenever he ruminated he became sad, but there was a day decreed for the end of this sadness too.

The next two to three years of his life were such that he had encounters with even more ruthless realities of life.

It was then that he talked to Shagufta at length and impressed upon her that he had now begun to accept each new bitter truth merely as another truth; he perceived natural and unnatural, all, as a preference; he believed in freedom of choice . . . and he had no right to object to anyone's private and personal choices. For a while, Shagufta expressed her wonder at hearing him. Her wonder morphed into laughter at Abdus-Salam's following sentence: 'I have grown up enough now to comprehend the reason for the divorce.' On hearing this, a mystical delight radiated from Shagufta's face, which transformed into a memorable laugh. Both of them kept laughing for a long time. There is a mention of this day in one of Abdus-Salam's diaries. After recounting this incident in detail, he has written: 'God has no gender.'

An enduring bond formed between Shagufta, Kulsum and him. He became their friend and confidant, a partner in their joys and sorrows. Several times, both of them told Abdus-Salam that the expression of self is not beholden to gender. He respected their way of life. A few years later still, when his expeditions into fiction became expansive, he professed to them: 'Merely being in a minority does not render any act unnatural.' He had already acknowledged Shagufta's spirit and courage in her personal life saying that in her past as well as progressing life, there was at least no fraud, treachery and deceit. During the same days, he fathomed the veiled impetuses behind Nazeer's disappearance. On recollecting the repugnant face of the madrasa's imam, he would become enraged. He would feel that had he been aware of such matters earlier, he would have peeled off that imam's beard.

Little by little, the truth of the relationship between Shagufta and Kulsum dawned upon the members of the family too, and all of them turned away from the two. After a few years, Abdus-Salam's aunt too departed this world. After her death, Shagufta was absolutely alone. Relatives had anyway severed their ties earlier. At this tragic juncture, Abdus-Salam looked after her with exemplary care. He would visit the village a couple of times a year, carrying gifts and other useful things for Shagufta. He would chat a lot with Kulsum too, and each time, he would remind her how she used to glare at him.

The firmness with which the threads of the hearts of these three stayed intertwined throughout their lives presents a truly exceptional instance.

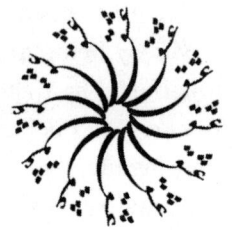

An intriguing thought would occur to Abdus-Salam on observing the women of his village and its rivers; it was a thought which, in a comprehensive order, was shaped thus in his mind one day: 'The suffering of Konkani women and rivers is one and the same.' This sentence is inscribed in his personal diary in a long paragraph about his village.

The year in which he passed his twelfth-grade exams, he went to Konkan for recreation and amusement during the summer holidays. This time, he stayed in Konkan for two months. He called on all his relatives and almost all the people in the village. He would visit houses in the village, spend some time there, and just observe life. How could he have known that whatever he was witnessing had the potential of becoming the material for fiction one day! Villagers, at that point, had abandoned farming. The land had been handed over to the adivasis (natives) for tilling, and in recompense, a portion of the harvest would go to the landowner. Some tracts of land on which no crops were sown for several years shed tears at the negligence and injustice of their owners, as they got soaked in rain. Abdus-Salam remembered, his female relatives would embrace him with affection earlier when he visited the village. They would kiss his forehead; would shower blessings on him. But now, children do not have the good fortune of being accorded such closeness. So much so that sons have unequivocally explicated the difference of confidant (*mahram*) and non-confidant (*namahram*) from the textbook of *Jama'at ul-Jama'at* even to women who are close to death. Now, even shaking hands (with women) is likened to a form of 'fornication', and people have been duped into believing that for a thousand years, that particular portion of the hand will keep burning in the raging fires of hell.

Fires of hell and torment of the grave have become themes of daily conversations and debates. All around, madrasas have sprung up imparting instruction in *fiqh* (jurisprudence) and *maslak* (rules of conduct). The boys who are customarily vagrant, or the girls who, after their first menstrual period, dare to eat *karonda* fruits or pick up many-coloured pebbles from the edge of the riverbed by vaulting the fences of their houses, are instantly dressed in black garments and admitted to madrasas to acquire instruction in ethics and character-building.

After being discharged from the madrasas, these girls are called *aalima* (learned); they are regarded with respect. Abdus-Salam met one such aalima during these summer holidays. He had gone to meet a distant relative at his house. It turned out that the gentleman was not at home, and his daughter, the aalima, was alone in the house at that time. Abdus-Salam spent some time talking to her, and this meeting turned out to be quite pleasant. The aalima knew in which relative's house he was lodged. Now whenever her parents made for the bazaar, she would call and invite Abdus-Salam over. He too would cordially appear at her abode. There was a mixed hue of learning and religious faith in the aalima's conversation. Abdus-Salam was impressed by her. He liked the tea prepared by the aalima, and praised it freely. The aalima was pleased.

Once, it was around two in the afternoon. Abdus-Salam had just spread himself on the bed for a siesta after a meal of jackfruit *sabzi*, when the phone started ringing. He picked it up. The aalima's voice came through from the other side. After talking for two to three minutes, the aalima invited him to her house. When he arrived at her door, it was latched from outside. Abdus-Salam opened the latch and entered.

'Abida . . .'

'Arre, you are here! Come in, come to the padi.'

'Okay.'

'Latch the door before you come. It is quite windy.'

Following the aalima's instructions, he stuck his hand out from the window contiguous to the door, latched the door from the outside, and then shut the window. He went to the padi. In one corner of the padi, there was a bathroom.

The entrance to the bathroom did not have a door; rather, it was covered with a curtain. He sat down on the threshold descending into the room. Three or four minutes must have passed when Abida's voice fell on his ears:

'There is a towel hanging on the rope over there; please hand it to me. I forgot . . .'

'Sure.'

From behind the curtain of the bathroom, a hand with shapely fingers emerged. Abdus-Salam handed her the towel. The touch of Abida's fingers, coursing through his fingers, rushed to his heart forthwith and merged with it. It was as if he had taken a swig of a fêted, heady wine. He felt a distinct kind of pleasure. Abida, donning a mauve-coloured imported maxi, appeared in splendour before him, drying her hair with the towel. (He had erased 'appeared in splendour' after writing it, and replaced it with 'came and stood'. After a second reading, as a remark, he wrote in green ink beneath the same phrase: 'A description infused with Persian and Arabic words appears attractive, but the possibilities of exaggeration and artifice increase manifold. How can one steer clear of these kafirs, words?). Anyway! But I do not know why I relished reading 'appeared in splendour'. Could the reason for it be that Abida was an aalima? Only God knows better the state of our hearts . . . But I was penning that Abida, donning a mauve-coloured imported maxi, appeared in splendour before him, drying her hair with the towel. Her hair reached her waist. It was so dense, that for a moment, Salam felt, wherever Abida spread them, night would descend at that spot.

After a while, they were in Abida's bedroom. Abida was applying olive oil to her hair, and simultaneously conversing with Abdus-Salam. From time to time, she would raise her eyes and look into Abdus-Salam's eyes as if she were searching for something in his eyes.

'Where has everyone gone?'

'To a village nearby . . .'

'When will they return?'

'Not tonight; they will come back tomorrow morning. They are attending a wedding over there.'

'So, you will stay alone?'

'Yes.'

'Don't you get scared?'

'Scared of what? Evil spirits do no come as far as the sound of the azaan reaches.' Abida emitted the words in one breath.

'Yes, that's true.' Voicing his agreement, Salam again looked at the palm of his hand on which the touch of Abida's wet fingers had ignited an oddly wonderful feeling. Abida was combing her hair in front of the mirror when her comb got entangled in her hair. 'Ouch,' she reflexively called out.

When Abdus-Salam extended his hand to extricate the comb, Abida said: 'The comb will become disentangled.' Saying this, she paused and looked into Salam's eyes. Salam was perplexed as to why she was looking at him in such a manner. Abida had a distinct way of gazing . . . as if those eyes were gazing at him from somewhere far away and were trying to draw him to her. Before Salam could pose a question, Abida completed the sentence: 'But what about the entanglement of the heart?'

Abida was standing so close to Abdus-Salam that the scent of her imported maxi was spreading to his nostrils. Abida's body was touching his. Abdus-Salam's reflection undulated in the mirror. His reflection first turned wheatish, then marine-blue, then azure, and then mauve in which a separate red colour of the veins could be discerned. This image of his was a first experience for him. Abida's hands were on his waist. She seemed to be in an ardent rush, like a monsoon river in Konkan. That moment, she had such fervour, such flow, such rapture that to traverse her would have been close to putting one's life at risk.

Abdus-Salam kept the comb aside and promised to come again that night. Abida, standing in the doorway, watched him gradually fade in the afternoon glare. Salam took off to the dense jungle instead of returning to his aunt's house. Right in the heart of the jungle is a pond called 'Maani'. A pond with cool, sweet water . . . Twenty to twenty-five years ago, tigers as well as other beasts of prey would go there at night to quench their thirst, but spreading settlements and increasing deforestation had compelled the animals to migrate. Drinking some water from the pond, Abdus-Salam moistened his throat, whose entire sap had been dried up by Abida's mysterious glances. When the sensation of the cool water ran down through his throat, a verdant surge was infused in him. He kept wandering in the woods for several hours. When he returned to his aunt's house, Shagufta made tea for him. A little while after having his tea, he said: 'I shall return late in the evening.'

For some time, he conversed with various people. Then little by little, his steps, instinctively, began to advance as a drunkard's towards a tavern. When he reached Abida's house, it was latched from outside, but now he knew the meaning behind it. On entering the house, he secured the latch on the outside, and after closing the window, also latched the door carefully from the inside. Waiting next to the door for a moment, he caught his breath, and then called out to Abida.

'Come on in.'

Abida lay on the bed. The room was washed in darkness. The window was shut. However, there was a faint light in the room, which came in through the skylight. The moment Abdus-Salam entered the room, she stood up. Smiling, she motioned Abdus-Salam to sit. He sat down, but she remained standing.

'Abdus-Salam, you did not feel bad . . .?'

'Why would I feel bad? We are friends . . .'

'Certainly, we are friends. Even then . . .'

For a while, both were silent. Then Abdus-Salam said: 'Please sit. Why are you standing?'

Abida sat close to him. Abdus-Salam put his hand on her shoulder. She looked at Abdus-Salam tenderly with love-filled eyes in which there was an expression of both desire and longing. Abdus-Salam was now prepared for this moment. His fingers began to gently circle around Abida's neck. How could he know that Abida had turned into kneaded wet clay at the thought and anticipation of this moment? Clay that was amenable to being transformed into any shape and form at all. From the time that Abdus-Salam had left promising that he would return that night, Abida had done nothing except imagine the moment of his arrival repeatedly; except evoke the warmth and intensity of that moment in her mind. There was illimitable relish for her in this imagining, and this very pleasurable relish had transformed her body into kneaded clay. All she needed now was gentle warmth. Salam's fingers traced a circle on her neck, and in that circle, he was writing something but he himself could not fathom what he wanted to write. This caress radiated a fiery ripple within Abida's bosom. The kneaded clay was kindled. The colour of her eyes began to change. The imagination of desire became restless for the fulfilment of desire. Her lips became parched; she felt thirsty but did not want to get up to drink water. She wanted to become an ocean herself. She wanted to become the water raining from the skies. She wanted to become a river flowing torrentially. Salam put his hand on her lips. She kissed the palm of his hand with her tongue. At this, there was a rush in her heartbeat, and the blood in her veins, becoming restless, began searching for that singular apex where the agitated surge of blood transmutes to essence of camphor . . . due to which, the soul's melody suffuses the body as a fragrance; peers out of the body. To be intoxicated by this melody was Abida's longing, and Abdus-Salam had recognized this longing in her eyes; now he was sensing it in her entire body. Abdus-Salam's hand, making circular caresses, cascaded to Abida's breasts. Abida began to rub her legs against Abdus-Salam's legs. Abdus-Salam turned her face to his. Gazing into her eyes, he wished to read the state of her heart, but then, who can say why, Abida evaded meeting his eyes. She rested her neck on Abdus-Salam's shoulder.

When Abdus-Salam gently ran his fingers through her hair, Abida, in some unbridled rapture, kissed both his eyes. That night Abdus-Salam realized how imperative repeated and regular rains were for an uninterrupted flow and rush in rivers . . . or how fatefully indispensable their bond was with the succession of snowy mountains melting somewhere far away. In this regard, the rivers of Konkan are unfortunate. Most 'rivers' in Konkan are deprived of a heady surge throughout the year. Yes, in the rainy season, they flow to the brim, rolling, swaying and singing, but for most of the year, they remain parched, expectant and desolate. Their anguish can be gleaned solely by gazing into the eyes of the expectant, unhappy and lonely women of Konkan.

After a few years, making her closest friend privy to this secret, Abida revealed: 'Shutting my eyes, I wanted to feel the fire that had ignited in my body. It was the first time that my heart had surrendered to a boy. I was frightened, but my heart desired to love him regardless. When he touched me, I felt that there was something in me that was raring to explode like a bomb.' On hearing the word 'bomb', her friend laughed at first, and then said: 'Are you inferior to an atom bomb even today?!' Abida smiled at this flattery. Just then her friend informed her that she had seen on the TV yesterday that there had been bomb blasts at two or three places in Mumbai. Abida instantly quipped: 'It was not me; it was some other bomb.' Both of them giggled for some time at this witticism. After their laughter had abated, Abida related extensively the particulars of her sexual dissatisfaction to her friend, saying that she did not wish for any girl from the village, whose desire and longing were intense, to marry a man who was far away, employed in some distant country.

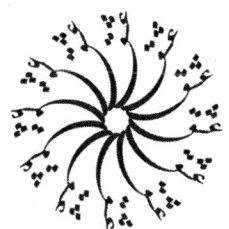

That night, he was with Abida until eleven. After their lovemaking, Abida prepared food for him. After eating, they made love twice.

Three years after this encounter, Abida got married to a boy from the village who was employed in Qatar. He would get a two-month leave every two years; after spending those two months at home, he would return to Qatar. At such times, Abida would miss Abdus-Salam a lot, and when her heart became too heavy, she too would take off towards the jungle where there was 'Maani'. One sip from it slaked all thirst. Whenever Abdus-Salam came to the village, he would wait for Abida at that very spot, and it was there that they would merge the sorrow of unfulfilled lives into the music of bodies in each other's arms. This intermittent union carried on for twenty-two years. Then, when afflictions of blood pressure and sugar consumed Abida's husband, and he returned to the village forever after leaving his job, Abida, confined to taking care of her husband, forgot the lush landscapes of intoxicating rain. In this entire course, Abida gave birth to two sons and a daughter. After several years, when Abida's eldest son, at one turn, appeared in front of Abdus-Salam for the first time, Abdus-Salam curiously felt as if he was looking at the image of his own young self. There are many other anecdotes of this love preserved in one of the chapters in Abdus-Salam's diary, which he has not included in the 'Saga of Passion'.

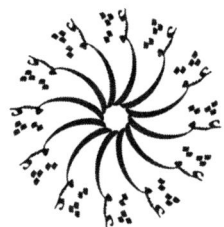

Abdus-Salam was fond of making excursions and travelling. Frequently, he would make programmes for picnics with his friends. In his view, the pollution, filth and uproar of urban life could be alleviated by spending time in the lap of green leafy valleys, the natural environment, mountains and waterfalls. The monotony of life, restating the same deliberated banalities in day-to-day interactions to the same individuals but not feeling repetitive and not becoming heartbroken by the state of numb dejection arising out of all this, signified the 'loss of self' for Salam.

Most of his friends were in accord with his view, and all of them together made frequent trips to spend time at outlying destinations. He had given strict warning to his friends that whenever they went on such excursions with the purpose of recreation, no one should bring up conversations about schools, the education system and the role of the teacher in shaping the future of students; otherwise, the pleasure of recreation would be lost. He was extremely attached to hilly locations, and to the life of adivasis settled around riverbanks and dense forests. The reason for this attachment and love was not that he was committing the folly of romanticizing their lives as 'fascinating lives'. On the contrary, he was crushed at their distraught condition, destitution, political and economic exploitation . . . at their shrivelled lives. The emaciation of their bodies, the emptiness in their eyes, the misery of their children and the half-nakedness of their women, they all shuddered in his chest. He wanted to protest against the miserable condition of these people, but making protest was not so easy when one was a government employee. He found this helplessness as baneful as an unhealed wound on the neck.

Once, he was visiting with three friends a place called Saphale, around sixty to seventy kilometres from Mumbai. The heat was intense; they were thirsty, and their supply of bottled water was over. A little way ahead, they spotted two huts constructed of mud and dry bush. At a further distance, there were about fifteen to twenty rough-and-ready houses too, but Abdus-Salam thought water would be available in the huts too. All four reached one of the huts made of cracked mud. The door of the hut was a ramshackle arrangement of wood and twigs.

'Hello, is there someone in there?'

'Is there someone around?'

A feeble voice asked from inside: 'Who are you looking for?'

'Arre, come out. We have come from the city.'

A weak, frail man stepped out.

'What do you want, sahib?'

'Do you have water?'

The bewilderment on the face of the frail man was plainly visible. He scanned all four of them with probing eyes. Scratching his head, he said: 'What did you say, sahib?'

'We want water. For drinking.'

The bewilderment on his face suddenly disappeared. A smile: a smile lush with life's elation . . . rushed to his dried up, dark lips, throwing open the portals of his withered soul. A glow returned to his eyes, captive for ages in the crypt of the collective historical subconscious.

'One minute, sahib.' Saying this, he went inside the hut.

All four stood there, chatting among themselves.

After a while, bending his neck, when one of them looked inside the hut, he did not see anyone.

'Arre, that adivasi is not inside.'

Everyone peeked inside one after the other.

There was a door at the side of the hut too. He had exited from there and disappeared.

The four of them went to the back of the hut. He was nowhere to be seen.

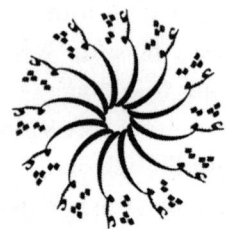

(After ten minutes.)

He was sprinting towards them from the direction of the rough-and-ready houses. His breathless, panting, dark silhouette was swaying on the footpath in the shimmering sunlight. That footpath must be no less than the bridge of reckoning for him.

All four of them were watching the silhouette turn into a man.

When he neared them, it seemed as if his frail ribcage had trapped too much air. He spoke: 'Sahib, excuse me. It took me a long time.'

There was a sack in his hand. He entered the hut with this sack and emerged with a pot the next moment. He took out two glasses from the sack.

All four of them turned into astounded spectators.

Rinsing the glasses, he offered them water.

Abdus-Salam and one of his friends drank the water and returned the glasses.

Abdus-Salam was stunned to see that the adivasi's eyes, dried up since ages, were moist with an imperceptible trace of a tear. Who knows for how many ages had this moistness, this water inside him, gathered as clouds!

Abdus-Salam placed a hand on his shoulder. A mild shudder coursed through his frail body, and those clouds burst. He started to cry vehemently.

The four of them stood dazed.

At last, Abdus-Salam asked him: 'Why are you crying?'

He remained silent.

He asked him again, but he kept quiet.

'Arre, what happened?' another friend asked.

'Sahib, no one drinks water from our hands. Today, for the first time in my life, I have had the opportunity to serve you water. It is a miracle; you consider me human . . . I am overjoyed.' He spoke in a voice choked with emotion.

Abdus-Salam had gauged the situation. The never-ending loneliness and solitude that centuries of exploitation and inequality had forced into this adivasi's existence was for the first time today, even for a moment, enlivened and invigorated. Someone had asked something of him as a human; otherwise, members of the upper castes remained at a distance from the adivasis' houses, their utensils . . . even their shadows. For this reason, in a surge of joy, he had taken off for the hamlet of the adivasis where a couple of people used glasses. He himself drank water out of a plastic cup. On such a memorable day of his life, how could he have offered them water in a plastic cup!

After a pause, Abdus–Salam said to him: 'Baba, it would have been quite all right even if you had given us water in the pot.'

They sat with him for a long time. They listened to his stories, tales of the forest, accounts related of the lives of people of inferior castes. They jotted down their address in Marathi on a piece of paper, telling him to look them up whenever he came to the city. But he never came to the city.

Whenever Abdus-Salam read in the newspapers about adivasis or poor farmers committing suicide due to starvation, the face of that adivasi with the weak, frail body would hover in front of his eyes. He used to ponder: 'Would he too have perished in the flames of starvation? Would starvation have driven him to suicide?'

Abdus-Salam would stare at the sky with mournful eyes. He couldn't say anything. How was a protest against centuries of inequality possible with words? In such oppressive moments, he would get out of the house. He would wander erratically in the crowds, would reach the Bismillah Paan Shop: 'Abid, a Bhola, katri supari, star mar kar.'

Could it be that the oppression and sadness within him was dispelled solely by consuming maava?

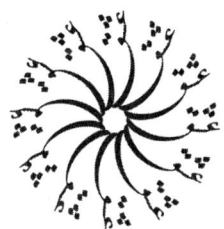

One day, at his school:

A programme under the auspices of 'Bazm-e-Adab' (Forum of Literature) was to take place at the school.

Abdus-Salam was interested in such activities. He considered it his responsibility to encourage and groom the creative abilities of students. He desired to participate in this programme with great fervour. This episode transpired during the early years of his teaching life. A selection of students was made. Different posts and duties in the literary association were delegated. The students too participated enthusiastically. Some creative write-ups were solicited for a wall-tableau. Three or four teachers who had no association with literature were also at the forefront in organizing the

event. Reputed writers and poets were contacted. After
the schedule of the programme was in place, the trustee was
apprised that a literary and cultural programme was being
arranged in the school, for which well-known personalities
were being invited. He would have to deliver the keynote
address. The trustee had no attachment to literary or cultural
programmes but despite that, he agreed immediately. Maybe
he assumed that this activity would benefit him somehow.
Even Salam did not have much familiarity with this man's
personality. Nevertheless! The Bazm-e-Adab programme
began and ended. The students listened to the verses of
the poets keenly, and with fervour. They obtained their
autographs. Salam noticed that day, what radiance suffused
the poets' faces as they handed out their autographs! A young
poet, who had given his first autograph, looked overjoyed.
After dinner, he needed to visit the toilet. Perched on
the toilet seat, he dreamily watched himself handing out
autographs so many times in the world of his imagination
that he dozed off. In his dream, he doled out autographs
to Amitabh Bachchan, Manmohan Singh, Rabindranath
Tagore, Allama Iqbal and Tarzan. All of them were waiting
in a queue to obtain autographs from him at the end of
an international mushaira. The last one in the queue was
Bahadur Shah Zafar. The colour of his autograph book was
greenish. The young poet cast one look at his beard, and
recited a couplet while signing the autograph book:

> *Khuddar hun kyun aaoon dar-e ahl-e karam par*
> *Kheti kabhi khud chal ke ghataa tak nahin aati*

(Self-respecting am I, to the door of benefactors why
should I come?
Never does a crop-field come crawling to the
clouds itself!)

After the mushaira, he was just about to join these great
figures for dinner when there was a knock on the toilet
door, and his dream lay shattered. The young poet sprang
out of the toilet. Two senior poets were facing him.

One of them said: 'Yaar, what were you doing in there
for half an hour?'

Rubbing his eyes, the young poet replied: '*Jo rahi so be-
khabari rahi* (All that remained was nothing but unawareness).'
And he proceeded nonchalantly to the exit.

The other senior poet, immediately checking him, said
mockingly: 'Respected sir, set your pyjama in order . . .
otherwise, the verse will spring out of your prosody.'

The young poet, in perplexity, turned his eyes to where
the senior poet's finger was pointing. All the intoxication of
'unawareness' evaporated instantly. In a state of abashment,
he turned away and adjusted his kurta-pyjama. In fact, he
had stuck a part of his kurta under the pyjama in his haste,
and he had forgotten to fasten a button of his pyjama.

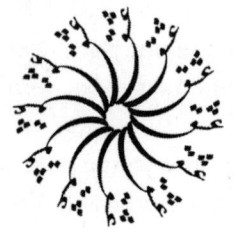

Before the mushaira commenced, the trustee made a protracted, tedious speech, which had no bearing at all on knowledge, education and practical life; on the contrary, it was a long-winded account of his proposals for the future through which his trust's financial state would be strengthened further. To conceal this oversight, he laid a lot of emphasis on the advancement of religious education. For a brief moment, Abdus-Salam felt that the man was truly a well-wisher of the people; that he wanted to embellish Muslims with adornments of education. Until then, he had no idea that individuals of such ilk turn on their faith-exuding persona solely to gratify their audience.

The wafting melodies of ghazals and the enthusiasm of the tabla beats had created a delightful atmosphere, but no perceptible change was visible in the emotions on the trustee's face. However, a shade of wonder was apparent on his face, which the old employees must have certainly encountered several times earlier.

After the programme, a meeting was held for the teachers and the members of the trust. Most teachers thought that the trustee would express his elation through words of encouragement at the success of the programme. After the guests left, everyone gathered in the staff room for the meeting, which was inaugurated with the recitation of verses from the Quran. The moment the recitation ended, the trustee exclaimed: 'I am a Muslim. My dream is to make good Muslims out of people through religious education. I hate all this poetry and stuff. It is against our religion. Are you guys hell-bent on spoiling the students?'

Abdus-Salam stared at him in disbelief.

A senior teacher spoke up: 'Poetry . . . is an irrevocable part of the culture of the Urdu language . . . and the curriculum.'

'How is behaving like kafirs in the name of language and culture exemplary religious conduct?' the trustee snapped with indignation.

A female teacher, whose husband was a poet, interjected: 'Sir, what has all this got to do with kafirs?'

'It *has* got to do with kafirs. All this is not a part of my religion.'

Abdus-Salam was on the verge of saying to the trustee that in his religion, a meeting where men and women were seated together was also forbidden . . . and all those means were forbidden too, through which he had acquired his wealth. But he could not say anything. He just kept listening to his seniors.

An Urdu teacher said, 'This way, the entire Urdu language will start belonging to kafirs.'

The trustee glared at him and said: 'I have opened an Urdu school because a maximum number of religious books are in that language. All of you, read religious books.'

Abdus-Salam was wondering whether this man had ever read a single book about religion in his entire life.

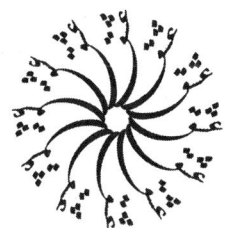

'I was not aware that religious books are not meant for reading, but for giving advice to others to read them.'

'Religion: it is not there to be practiced; rather, it is a shortcut for enhancing one's already inflated persona, and for achieving social status as well as political goals. Religion is merely a walking-staff, not vision.'

It is probable that Abdus-Salam jotted these observations in his 'diary of random notes' precisely in the background of the above episode. We also find some other thoughts that were entered in the diary at a date a year later; for instance: 'A large section of wealthy people uses religion as an intoxicating drug. Dishonest, self-seeking, bootlicking, fraudulent and immoral individuals too, donning the mantle of religiosity, try to disguise their murky hearts and festering mindsets. These people customarily deploy two or three Arabic phrases during the prelude as well as the conclusion of their speeches, because of which, ignorant and indigent Muslims are susceptible to committing the error of regarding these people as custodians of faith.'

It is possible to trace the eccentricity that had crept into Abdus-Salam's persona through reading about more such incidents, which he has recorded in his 'diary of random notes' in substantial detail. These incidents are spread over 330 pages!

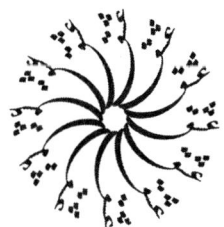

The well-shaft of his self:

Abdus-Salam was terrified of wells.

There is an incident from his childhood. He was playing with his friends. After a considerable while, a couple of them felt thirsty. With the intention of getting water, they all proceeded to a well. One of them would plunge the bucket into the well and draw water, and the other would drink it by cupping both his hands. When Abdus-Salam plunged the bucket into the well, the rope inadvertently slipped from his hands, and the bucket fell deep down into the well. Abdus-Salam tried to peek into the well to figure out where the bucket was . . . For what seemed like ages, he kept clutching the edge of the well, frozen and numb.

Finally, a friend of his tapped him and asked: 'Hey, what have you been peering at all this time?'

Startled, Abdus-Salam turned. The cavernous darkness of the well had plunged deep into his eyes.

Another friend said: 'No one has seen us. Let's scoot from here.'

Another said: 'Buckets keep slipping from hands . . . Why are you so worried? Someone else will come along and retrieve it.'

Abdus-Salam's friends tried to dispel the clouds of gloom that had suddenly cast a shadow over his face, but were not successful. Then, a friend of his jibed in a derisive tone: '*Abe*, was there a ghost in the well?'

Abdus-Salam turned to the friend who had made this jibe. Their eyes met. Due to sadness, there was a peculiar fortitude that had suffused Abdus-Salam's eyes. On discerning this, his friend lowered his eyes.

The other friend said: '*Saale*, will you say something or not?'

Abdus-Salam replied: 'The well was very deep. I have never seen a well so deep.'

One of them said: 'Don't spew out dialogues like in the movies.'

The other chimed in: '*Abe*, he is just whipping up suspense.'

Abdus-Salam was certain that no one would believe what he had seen in the well. And apart from him, no one would be capable of seeing what he had seen. That night, Abdus-Salam did not eat. Muttering some excuse, he retired to bed early. When he opened his eyes under the blanket, he was petrified. He felt he was in the well. There was darkness all around him. His gaze kept roving but there was no end to the depth of the well. As if the well was a never-ending tunnel. An endless, dark tunnel. And it was not the bucket that was swaying in the dark tunnel. It was perhaps his father's face. From where did his father's face appear in this tunnel? Red, flushed face, and large swollen eyes. A wide forehead on which there was not a single crease. Thin lips. Words were being expressed by those lips in the same disarrayed manner as when his father returned home totally smashed with alcohol and weed. And then . . . for no rhyme or reason, there would be a tumult in the house. The inebriation, in its concluding manifestation, would crash upon his mother. His mother's aggrieved face would be swollen due to his father's thrashings. Coincidentally, his mother's battered face too was suspended in a corner of the tunnel, which he noticed after some time.

And his elder brother's face, who, vexed and harassed by his father's tyranny, had run away from the house several times, but each time, love for his mother had brought him back in two or three days. That face was there too, on one side, pallid and distraught. He was truly perplexed today. From where did all the incidents that had occurred in his house appear in this dark well in a fraction? Only God knows! But those incidents had made him frightful. In an aggravated state, he talked to himself for some time, which he could not remember later.

He kept trying to bury these incidents in the quicksand of oblivion.

But the fact is that after this incident, a fear of wells possessed his soul. The well was the tale-bearer of the netherworlds of his tragic subconscious.

Abdus-Salam has alluded in his personal diary to the fact that he was extremely resentful of his father's alcoholism and wretchedness, due to which a hole had formed in his being into which he too would stare. In that restless darkness, he would have the distinct sensation of some things crawling, but he could never fathom who or what those things were. The degree to which his soul wanted to measure the depths and mysteries of the hole in his being, its circle was spreading and deepening further to the same degree. In that circle, he could look down on to the stony severity, distress and anxieties of his childhood memories. He could see his mother's dim eyes filled with desolation born of her husband's oppression. Sometimes, he felt that his mother's eyes would burst due to the intensity of pain, and the viscous matter from their innards would splatter on his face. The dreams that these eyes had nurtured, stagnating right there, had died, had rotted. He could smell the stench. He would see his mother's face, which had no eyes, where two dark stains could be seen in place of eye-sockets. But in those dead planets, there was a curious gravitational pull. All the objects around, on their own, fell into them and forfeited their existence . . . To terminate such feelings, he would wander around dazed, distraught and displaced for hours . . . Furthermore, there would be concerted attempts on his part to somehow forget the melancholy produced by the continual bitterness and discontent in the precincts of the house . . .

Ignored by his father to an agonizing limit, the tears not shed for this agony, drop by drop, kept dripping into the hole of his being. (The crucifixes of memories thrown into this deep, inner well shall become extinct with the force of time—this assumption of his was an enormous mistake.) Abdus-Salam thought that he was the world's most fortunate man who had a 'memory to forget'. Probably, this was the great paradox that divided his persona into two level compartments. He was aware that there was an invisible well in his heart, and he was also conscious that in a struggle to hide that fact, he kept himself submerged in myriad activities. Relationships, loves, conflicts and successes: in reality, they were excuses to avert his eyes from the soul's endless darkness. That is why he always kept himself active and occupied. Had he really forgotten that he was the graveyard of numerous realities? Why is it the fate of Man to turn into a dreadful cemetery of memories?

One day, seated with Safia in the National Park, when he was conversing about the subject of love and society, Safia had accosted him saying: 'Rather than whiling away time in chatter . . . there is an old well over there; come, let's go and see it.' In reply, this exclamation had spontaneously issued forth from his mouth: 'Even here; an old well!' That day, for a moment, he had realized that all the things he had forgotten were, in fact, the things that he remembered the most.

Safia did not pay any heed to this sentence. At that time, she was anyway not in a state to pay attention to anything. Holding Abdus-Salam's hand, and dragging him, she led him some distance away where the shrubbery was thicker. There was a tree casting dense shadows. They both sat down resting their backs against the trunk of the tree. Safia leaned her head on his shoulder and closed her eyes. Abdus-Salam cast a look around and enquired: 'You had said, there is a *banwdi* (stepwell) here. Where is it?'

Parting her eyelids, Safia replied in a whisper: 'Silly! You were lecturing on the topic of love . . . but you do not know even this much . . . Love is not a matter to be talked about, but something to be acted upon.'

Abdus-Salam smiled and responded in an undertone: 'My God! You seem to be an expert in matters of love.'

Safia replied in the Bombay vernacular, which meant: 'This is women's arena, and in these matters, we are way more practical.'

'And what are men?'

'Men! Women are of the opinion that they are experimental.'

After this brief exchange, Safia became practical and Abdus-Salam became experimental.

When Abdus-Salam committed Safia's narrative to his diary, he also annotated it with a remark about this episode. It read: 'If there were no love, Man, falling into the mysterious well of the heart, would die.'

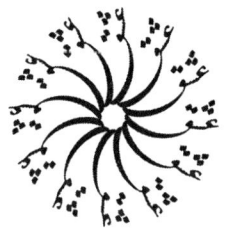

On the same page, he added another remark after six years: 'In such a lonely and meaningless life without God . . . what else can make things meaningful . . . except love? The smallest of the small and the most artificial of the artificial love too, maintains its flavour, its pleasure, its blossoming, and its colours. Devoid of this, existence too would become colourless and formless like God.'

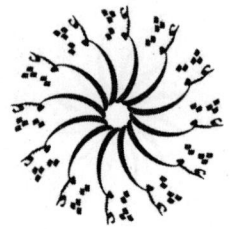

One such day also was to arrive when Abdus-Salam would have to confront the most deep-seated fear in his self. He would have to jump into a well . . . The core which was the source of his soul's anguish, which had turned his existence into a trial . . . into that abysmal hole, he would have to dive one day.

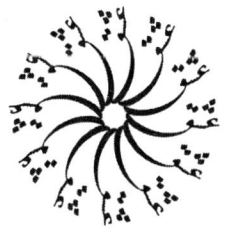

It so turned out that the school's farewell party was in progress. It must have been around six in the evening. The students were all quite charged and excited. Ghazals and film-songs were being sung; there were speeches. On the other end, in the open ground contiguous to the wall of the school, a female student was writing a last letter to her beloved. Perhaps her parents had arranged her marriage prematurely, against her wishes. Or her lover's heart had begun to throb for someone else. This student's visage was familiar to Abdus-Salam. When he absent-mindedly gazed down through the window, he spotted a silhouette moving in the twilight. He focused his eyes on the silhouette. He focused on it intently, and then, cast an impassive glance

over the students present in the programme. He was
surprised at not finding Ruhana among them.

Descending from the second floor, crossing the precincts
of the school, he began to walk rapidly in the direction where
he had spotted Ruhana's silhouette. There, at a distance, was
a well. In that duration, Ruhana slashed a finger of her left
hand with a sharp-edged blade, and wrote on a sheet of
paper with her freshly-spouting blood: 'Samad, you were
my world. I do not want to live in a world in which you are
not there. Goodbye.'

She placed the paper on the ground, and advanced
towards the well.

It was just when she reached the well that Abdus-
Salam spotted her. He instinctively ran towards her. But
by then, she had already jumped into the well. Abdus-
Salam probably did not have the time to shout and scream
to rush others to the well, and then implore someone to
jump into the well to save the girl. On reaching the well,
some occult force clasped him to the ground for a fraction.
He stopped. He found himself standing on the bridge of
reckoning of memory and forgetting. Suffused with the
suffering of the divine torment of the past, he called out
to other teachers in the school with a sky-severing cry,
and plunged into the well. His cry, knocking against the
windowpanes, resounded inside the programme hall.
Startled for a moment, the teachers and the students
dashed in the direction of the cry. During all this, holding
Ruhana on his shoulders in the seclusion of the well, and
stretching his head to the sky, Abdus-Salam was shouting
out to his friends.

Everyone rushed there.

Ruhana had not become unconscious; however, she had been rendered catatonic with outright bewilderment and disbelief. Right then, someone spotted the paper on the ground. Two of the female teachers lifted up Ruhana, and swiftly rushed her to the hospital. Abdus-Salam took a sip of water. After a while, he stood up. His steps lifted towards the well. Placing his hand on the edge of the well, he peered into it. His father's red, glowering face was undulating in a silvery darkness. In one corner, the sadness of his mother's dejected, weary eyes was in slumber. Today, looking into the well, he was even more amazed that along with the azure, sky-blue colours, one more face was rippling there; it was a face that he had loved boundlessly, but whose story he could never bring himself to commit to the pen. He realized that what he had thought was a well until today was not a well but his heart. The pit in which Ruhana had plunged; that was a well!

His eyes became moist.

He turned and squatted against the wall of the well. Due to the press of blood, his eyes were aglow like flames. With a crushing force, it dawned upon him that his life up till then had been nothing but a saga of self-adornment, and his acrimonious struggle with himself. This realization submerged him into an intensely tragic disposition, which irrevocably ripped open the unhealed wound of his heart. He wept inconsolably, but his eyes were parched for tears. At that time, he did not even have maava—Bhola, katri supari, star mar kar—with him in his pocket.

Three days after this episode, the police found him dead in his house. According to the medical report, his arteries had ruptured due to extremely high blood pressure, resulting in a brain haemorrhage. Even after his death, his eyes were wide open. After all, why was he so desirous of beholding the world? Who could ever know?

Scan QR code to access the
Penguin Random House India website